DANIEL'S WALK

MICHAEL SPOONER

HENRY HOLT AND COMPANY

NEW YORK

ACKNOWLEDGMENTS

Thanks to these consultants for their wisdom and encouragement (in chronological order): Sylvia, Nancy, Ona, Katie, Bob and Molly, Tait, Caitlin, and F.H.E. Thanks to Zan. Thanks to Reka. Thanks to Barre for the phrase. Thanks to all of these. *Mi takuye oyasin.* They did their best with me; the shortcomings of the story are of course my own.

Henry Holt and Company, LLC, *Publishers since 1866*
115 West 18th Street, New York, New York 10011
www.henryholt.com

Henry Holt is a registered trademark of Henry Holt and Company, LLC
Copyright © 2001 by Michael Spooner
All rights reserved. Distributed in Canada by H. B. Fenn and Company Ltd.

Library of Congress Cataloging-in-Publication Data
Spooner, Michael.
Daniel's walk / Michael Spooner.
p.   cm.
Summary: With little more than a bedroll, a change of clothes, and a Bible,
fourteen-year-old Daniel LeBlanc begins walking the Oregon Trail in search of his
father who, according to a mysterious visitor, is in big trouble and needs his son's help.
1. Overland journeys to the Pacific—Juvenile fiction. [1. Overland journeys to the
Pacific—Fiction. 2. Oregon National Historic Trail—Fiction. 3. Frontier and pioneer
life—West (U.S.)—Fiction. 4. Robbers and outlaws—Fiction. 5. West (U.S.)—
Fiction.] I. Title.
PZ7.S7638 Dan 2001   [Fic]—dc21   00-69559

ISBN 0-8050-7543-7 / EAN 978-0-8050-7543-4
1   3   5   7   9   10   8   6   4   2

First published in hardcover by Henry Holt and Company in 2001
First paperback edition—2004 / Book design by David Caplan
Printed in the United States of America on acid-free paper. ∞

This book is for Isaac.

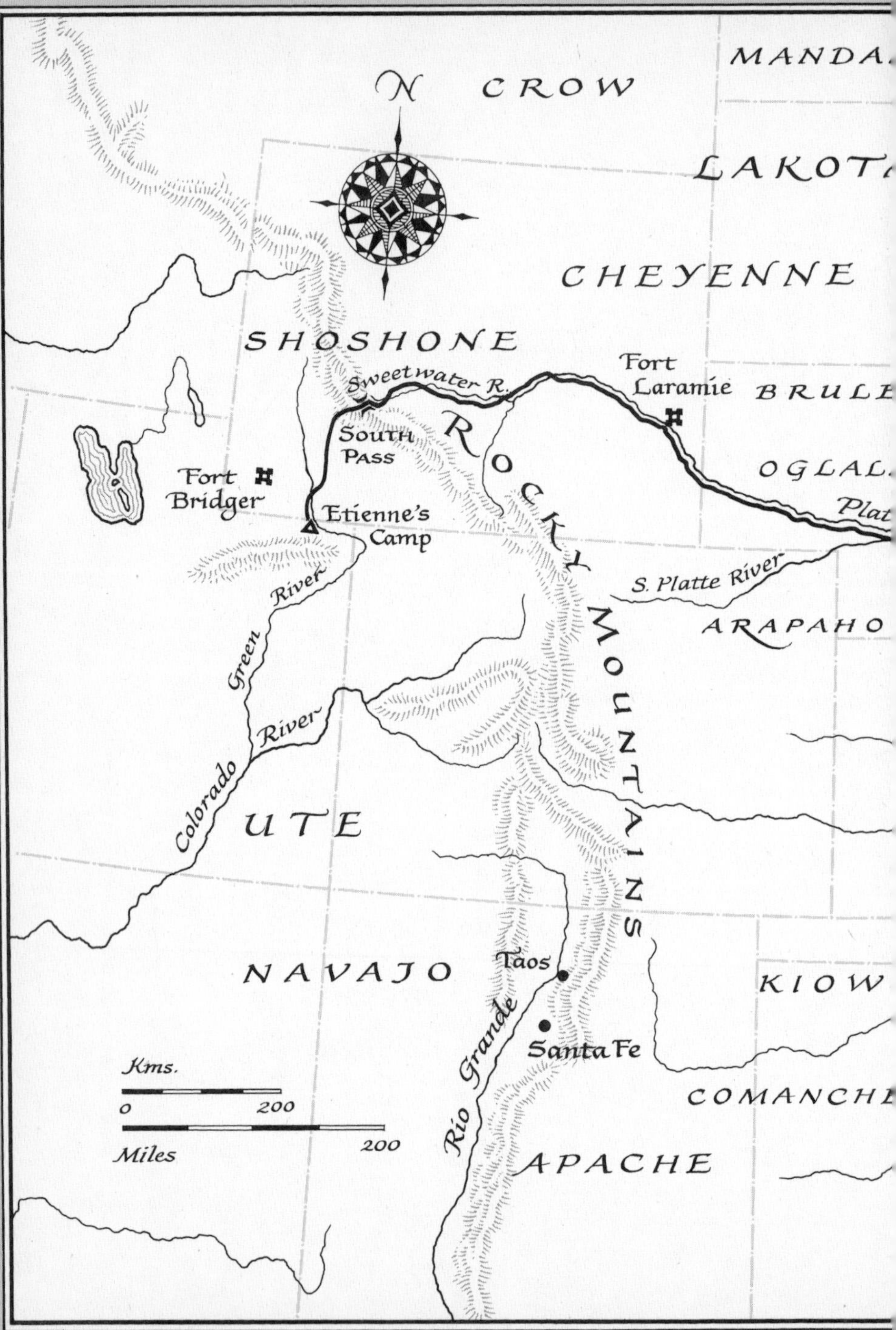
N
CROW
MANDA
LAKOTA
CHEYENNE
SHOSHONE
Sweetwater R.
Fort Laramie
BRULE
South Pass
ROCKY MOUNTAINS
OGLALA
Fort Bridger
Etienne's Camp
Plat
S. Platte River
Green River
ARAPAHO
Colorado River
UTE
NAVAJO
Taos
KIOW
Rio Grande
Santa Fe
Kms.
0
200
COMANCHE
Miles
200
APACHE

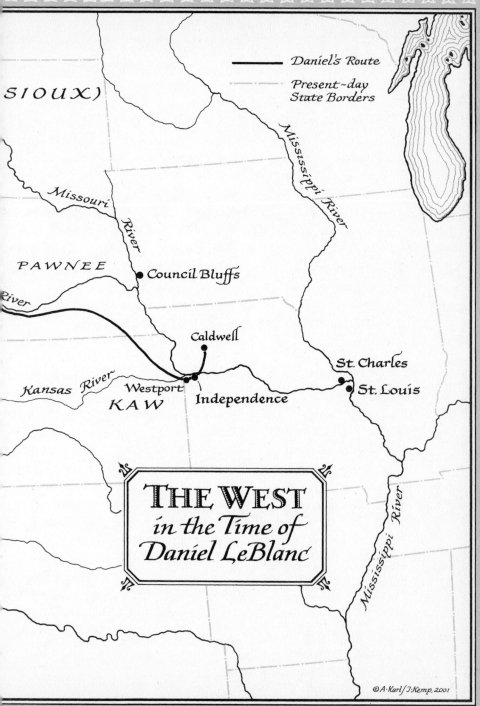

Daniel's Route

Present–day
State Borders

(SIOUX)

Mississippi River

Missouri River

PAWNEE

• Council Bluffs

River

Caldwell
•

• St. Charles

Kansas River

Westport

KAW

Independence

• St. Louis

THE WEST
in the Time of
Daniel LeBlanc

Mississippi River

©A·Karl/J·Kemp, 2001

Contents

Distance was the enemy, not Indians or crossings or weather or thirst or plains or mountains, but distance, the empty, awesome face of distance. . . . There was no end to it, not even any shortening. Morning and night it was there unchanged, hill and cloud and sky line beyond reach or reckoning.

—A. B. GUTHRIE,
The Way West

PART ONE

Caldwell, Missouri

One

"GIT UP, BOY!" A fierce whisper in my ear, and a claw digging at my shoulder.

"Git up! I got one word to say, and I ain't got much time." It was a thin voice, dry and old and whiskery. I could hear it, but I couldn't get my eyes open. I figured I was dreaming.

"Who are you?" I croaked.

"That don't matter. Just you listen here, and I'll be gone."

I shoved my face hard into the pallet.

"Yessir," I moaned. "I'm listening." Dreams dragged at me, but the claw held on.

"Your daddy's in trouble, boy," said the Voice. "I've did for him the best I could, but, truth to tell, I got troubles of my own. Now I've tracked you down, and it's up to you from here, son."

Swirls of dreams, snaggled branches, lightning and blizzards.

"You hear me, boy?" the Voice hissed. "Your daddy. Trouble. You know how to find him?"

I was torn between dream and dream, and the Voice troubled me. The claw shook my shoulder once again.

"Yessir," I managed. "I'll see to it, first thing."

"You do that." The claw went away, and then it was back.

"Listen," said the Voice. "Clements is set to go out again; he'll help you. Now you got to forget you ever saw me. Hear?"

"Yessir, I will."

"If you ever did saw me, that is."

Two

MORNING SWAM through the haze on the river; it was hardly cooler than midday. The air was thick, and I could hear the flies already buzzing at the cooking pots. In this weather, sleep is never restful.

I levered myself to a kneeling position and felt around for my shirt. I stepped into my trousers. My aunt and uncle slept in the back room of the cabin; my pallet was always out here in the front. I rolled it up with a foot and shoved it over by the wall, near the small chest that held all my worldly things. I rubbed my eyes till I could almost see. My head felt thick.

"Bucket's empty." This is what passed for conversation with my Aunt Judith—her hard voice around a cold fact. Never a request, never an order; she just liked to hint, if you could call it that. She was not unkind, but somehow she had forgotten how to be happy. Life was a burden to her, as she was fond of saying. And she believed that boys were put on earth to do farm chores and memorize the scriptures. I had done plenty of both since we moved here.

She rapped the bucket two quick ones with a wooden spoon, and went back to stirring something in a bowl.

"Yes ma'am, I'll get it," I said.

I wondered if it was hazy and humid like this everywhere in May. What was it like in the Rocky Mountains, where my pa was trapping and hunting? I thought it was probably bright and clear, with blue skies and creeks that splashed and laughed their way down from the mountains. Not like this creek here—so slow and gray, it might as well give up and just be mud.

Uncle John and I had found a spring up the hill from the creek bank, and we had dug it out and lined it with stone to make a sort of well. This water was cool and clear, even in the worst days of summer. I dragged the bucket through the surface and brought it up. I splashed my face and ran my fingers through my hair before turning back toward the cabin.

It's hard to see your face in a bucket of water, but what I could see startled me. I was looking more like my pa every day; maybe that was why Aunt Judith was always so cross. I could see his dark eyes in my face, his black hair hacked off and shoved behind my ears, and the chin that came out too far, squared off too sharply. He wanted to name me Etienne, after himself, but my mother made him settle for Daniel. I think it was French enough to please him, but English enough to get by her side of the family. Like Aunt Judith.

I set the bucket on the table, and my aunt said, "There's tea; John will be back for morning prayer and biscuits in ten minutes." I poured tea in a crockery cup and took it outside to the stump where I always went to think. I sat for a moment listening to Uncle John splitting wood behind the cabin.

From here, I could look down at the wagon road that skirted the base of our hill. More of a long, skinny clearing than a road, I thought: two wheel ruts through the black dirt. The town of Caldwell was a mile north of us. Southeastward, about two days' walk, the road ran to Fort Orleans, on the Missouri River, and then tracked the river all the way to St. Louis. But most people going to St. Louis would book passage on the steamboat. To the southwest, the road found Westport and Independence, where the trappers' pack trains used to gather before they set out across the plains to the Rockies or to Santa Fe.

My pa said the road broke out of the trees near the Kansas River and then ran over the High Plains for seven hundred miles. Finally it stumbled into the Rockies, where the wild-game trails lay like a web over the mountains. Lately some trappers had become guides for caravans of wagons making the same trip. Settlers were going west from here all the way to Oregon and California, gouging the trail deeper and wider as they went. My pa despised the wagons. He had no use for towns or farms, for cobblestones or digging in the earth. "These people are *cochons*," he always said. "Pigs, rooting in their own mess."

When I leaned down to set my cup on the ground, I saw a footprint. Strange to see a track I didn't know. This one had a soft outline, rounded at both the heel and the toe—a moccasin track. It wasn't mine; I did have moccasins, but I'd been barefoot since April. And it wasn't John's, I knew, because my uncle never went without his boots. He even slept in them some nights.

A moccasin. But we hadn't seen an Indian here in months, and the only other men who wore moccasins were the old free trappers like my pa.

I stood up. The Voice. *Your daddy. Trouble.* Suddenly my hands were shaking. I squeezed my eyes shut and clapped my palms over my ears. *I've did for him the best I could. It's up to you from here, son.*

A few yards down the slope, I found two more tracks—two softly rounded imprints pointing toward the cabin, where the old man must have stood for a moment, just looking. A step farther, I found one last one, leading away.

Three

A HICKORY ROD came down across my knee with a thwack.

"Mr. LeBlanc, please pay attention. Thank you."

"Sorry, sir. I don't know where my mind is today."

"Evidently not in school, Mr. LeBlanc. However, your body is so seldom with us lately that when you do choose to appear in school I must insist you bring your mind along as well."

"Yessir."

"Such as it is."

"Sir?"

"Miss Pritchard, the word is 'independence,' if you please."

"Yessir. 'Independence': i-n-d-e-p-e-n-d-e-n-c-e. *Noun.* The state or quality of separateness; nondependency; self-reliance and self—um—self-sufficiency."

"Not bad. And your sentence, Miss Pritchard?"

"Yessir: 'The thirteen colonies won independence from the king of England.'"

"Yes, indeed. Now, Mr. Canfield, the word 'wilderness,' if you please—spelling, usage, and a sentence."

"Yessir. 'Wilderness': w-i-l-d-e-r-n-e-s-s. *Noun*. Forest, plain, or mountain not yet settled nor put to the uses of civilization. Sentence: 'The joy of every citizen is to subdue the wilderness before us.'"

"And the wilderness within as well, Canfield, or so one would hope. Mr. Davis, your word is 'savage.'"

"Uh, yessir. 'Savage': er, s-a- . . . um . . . v- . . . i-d-g-e? Er. *Verb*? Meaning wild and . . . um . . . men of red skin, who murder the . . . ah, um . . . and . . . and sometimes eat their own children?"

"Mr. Davis, where I come from in Massachusetts, there is a story of a red man who taught the settlers how to plant and properly cultivate corn. In so doing, he saved an entire village from sure disaster. Now, would you call that man a savage?"

"Hmm? Oh yessir, they's all thieving savages."

"Sit down, Davis. Someone else: Miss Harris?"

"'Savage': s-a-v-a-g-e. *Adjective*. Not domesticated or brought under control; fierce, wild, or brutal. Sentence: 'The shepherd boy's crook struck down the savage wolf.'"

"Thank you, Miss Harris. Boys, crooks, and wolves. There's a lesson there, somewhere, I do not doubt. Now, Miss Sanborn, the word is 'loyal.'"

"Yessir. 'Loyal': l-o-y-a-l. *Adjective*. Unswerving in allegiance, faithful to one's lawful government, family, race, or friend to whom fidelity is due. Sentence: 'The son was loyal to his father's will.'"

"Fine, and thank you, Miss Sanborn. Mr. LeBlanc!"

I stumbled to my feet.

"Yessir!"

"The word is 'destiny,' if you please."

Four

DESTINY. NOUN. A course of events laid out by God or fate, from which there is no swerving.

I sat at the table with Aunt Judith. Her jaw was set, her small hands were clenched, and she wouldn't look at me. She seemed about to explode.

"He's in trouble," I said.

"You don't know that. You had a dream."

"Aunt Judith, I heard a voice in the night. And I saw fresh moccasin tracks around the cabin. I'm sure it was someone who came to tell me he's in trouble."

"Well, it's not like Etienne LeBlanc has been a great help when *we* had trouble, is it?" she replied, raising one eyebrow. I let that go. I kept my hands busy repairing a split in my pack frame. I was wrapping it with *babiche*, strips of wet rawhide; when they dried, the frame would be stronger than ever.

"Aunt Judith," I said again, "he's my father."

She smacked the table with her open palm.

"As if that means anything to him!" she snapped. "As if he's been here to raise you! Gone ten months a year to the mountains, when he ought to be right here putting down roots for you, if not for himself. When he ought to be right here with farm and family, teaching you to be a man, instead of a dreamer."

"Aunt Judith . . ."

"I swear, Daniel, I can't imagine what you're thinking. Let's just suppose you actually don't get killed and you don't get lost. Suppose you do find him, then what? Eh? Then you spend the next ten years scalping people and sullying your dead mother's memory with some Indian woman? Like he does?"

I'm sure I hadn't seen her cry since my mother died ten years ago, but the tears stood in her eyes now, and her cheeks were flushed. She groaned and looked away.

"Daniel," she said in a whisper. "All I have ever needed was my family, and my family has been taken from me one by one." I held still and she turned to me again. She smoothed her apron carefully with both hands, and then she spoke.

"My parents had eight children. First was Emily, your blessed mother, and I was second. Then came the twins, and then we lost four different babies to whooping cough and cholera. Still, the twins lived, praise God, and Mother specially doted on them. We all did. But when they were fourteen, the smallpox took Jacob, and straightaway Tom went daft. He got in trouble with the law and disappeared. With her four babies in the ground and both twins gone, poor Mother, she couldn't stand it. She turned her face to the wall and died feeble minded. Daddy just didn't know what to do without her, so he died, too. Do you see what I'm saying, Daniel? Before I was sixteen years old, my family of ten was down to two lonely orphans—your mother and me."

I had never met these people she named, but they were all my relatives, as well as hers. And they were all dead. I felt her loneliness deeply, and my own.

"Through it all, Daniel, your mother was my rock; she was sister and brother and mother and father to me, and, oh, how I loved her, how I looked up to her." Aunt Judith paused and sucked in a ragged breath. "Then she went and died, too."

It was too much to take in. I was quiet, keeping my hands busy. Aunt Judith was telling me this to keep me at home, but I think my mind was made up in that moment to go. My only close kin left was my pa, and I was bound to find him or die trying.

She smacked the table once again.

"Daniel, you're fourteen, and you have no idea what the world is like. Look at me: I am a woman twenty-nine years old with no parents, no brother or sister. And you know there's something wrong with me or John that we could never make a child of our own. Every blood relation I have ever had in this world has been taken, and you alone are all that's left." Her voice cracked.

"I am so angry, Daniel," she whispered. "I feel like Job's wife. If anything happens to you, I swear I will curse God and die."

We sat a moment in silence. I reached across to touch her forearm with my fingertips.

"I'll be careful, Aunt Judith. And I'll come back."

She squeezed my fingers with a wet hand. A strand of bright hair had fallen across her cheek, and she tucked it slowly back into place. She stood up without looking at me.

"There's jerked venison and biscuits," she said softly. "Nothing else will keep in this weather."

Five

I<small>N THE END</small>, it seemed so easy. I rolled my bedding, then slid my Bible, my heavy shirt, and canvas broadfall trousers into my pack. My flint and steel were in the pouch, along with plenty of shot and patch. My powder horn was full.

I didn't have the supplies on all the promoters' lists of necessaries: two pair of heavy brogans, two yoke of oxen, casks for water, rain gear, flour and salt and jerked beef. Sugar and trade blankets. But, then, a lot of people heading out the Oregon Road didn't have them either, and they seemed to make it.

Aunt Judith gave me biscuits wrapped in oilcloth. I took venison from the smokehouse. I put in a small steel trap, a length of cord, tied my bedroll to the bottom, and wrapped it all in a square of smoky canvas that might serve for a lean-to.

I wore my boots and packed the moccasins; the pack was lighter that way. I had two knives and the flintlock rifle; the rifle was old but it was short, dark, and solid. Like me.

My plan was simple: I would take the wagon road west from Independence. In a few days, I thought, I could catch up to the last group of emigrants who had passed through. I didn't think they would turn away a working volunteer. Otherwise, I figured I could walk as far as the crossing of the Kansas River in a couple of weeks and hire on with another group there.

I wasn't sure how long it would take to cross the High Plains, but probably all summer. When we reached Fort Bridger, I would start out alone again. *Follow the Green River south,* my pa had told me, *and then you're in my favorite territory.*

It would be cold in winter; my pa says Missouri has never dreamed the snow they have every year in the Rockies. But by then I might have a buffalo robe to wear, or I could swap something at a trading post for a trapper's wool capote.

I'm a good walker. If the weather was good, I figured, I could put miles behind me in a few short days.

Six

THE WEATHER was not good.

I skirted Independence in a light drizzle and crossed the river at Westport. I had no use for the barkers and hawkers of a trailhead town, and I didn't want to take the chance of being set on by thieves. Aunt Judith always said that where trappers, rivermen, Indians, and muleskinners all came together over a jug of rum, the devil himself couldn't be far away. When she said things like this, somehow I always felt all the evil of the world was my own personal fault.

"A young person traveling alone is a temptation that few such men can resist," she warned me many a time, "and if there's trouble, you will find no Good Samaritan along the low road through Independence, Missouri."

Directly to the west of Independence, I found the recent imprints of a large wagon caravan heading away through mud and the tall, wet prairie grass. Mule shoes had pressed heavy half-moons, and the iron rims of wagon wheels sank an inch or two into the damp earth. My spirits lifted in spite of the drizzle. They were two days ahead of me, I judged, but I could walk them down in three.

On my third night out, the moon rose into a fat black thunderhead. Lightning broke over the hills to the south of my camp, and I counted four seconds before the thunder reached me. I turned on my side and wormed into the corner of the lean-to as far as I could. Damp, bent-over bluestem grasses were my pallet and pillow. An ant danced over my wrist. I slept.

Thunder woke me. The rain was coming down in heavy slaps on my shelter, and I could see that things were only going to get worse. I tucked the rifle under the blanket on my uphill side and tried to go back to sleep.

Thunder again, and now the rain was coming down with serious purpose. My lean-to was soaked and sagging. I ventured a toe out from under the blanket and felt a cold puddle where my boots were supposed to be. I sat up.

I had chosen this little draw between two low hills because it looked sheltered from the wind and because there was plenty of firewood. Now I could see that it caught the rain like a tin scoop, and I was at the bottom. Rain was running off the hills in rivulets, soaking toward my camp from two directions, and filling my shelter with wet misery.

I emptied my boots and pulled them on. I hated boots even when they were dry, but this was easier than trying to carry them in a rainstorm. Thunder pounded my ears again, and then I heard the horses. Lots of them.

I snatched the rifle, pouch, and pack, and headed up the left side of the draw at a waterlogged trot. My hat flopped around my head like a soggy flower, and the blanket was still draped over my shoulders. I climbed the hill and found an oak for shelter. Its leaves thrashed above me in the wind, and the rain tore at my blanket. The horses came closer—about a dozen of them, I guessed. But why they were coming, and why tonight, I couldn't guess. In thirty seconds, they were crashing past my lean-to, stumbling, churning the mud to thick soup. Then I heard a whistle and a shout and two riders came into view. One of them spotted me and reined hard, as if he'd seen a ghost; his horse scrambled to keep its feet in the mud. Then lightning opened the sky and I saw my shadow clear as noon on Sunday. It nearly spooked me, too.

The silhouette of my blanket stood out like a torn black wing, and my hat made an ugly beaked shape on the ground. I saw myself as a bird blown through the world, and then the darkness slammed down again.

Seven

"**H**AGGARD! Your mount spooked? Let's go!" I could make out the second rider now; he pulled up beside the first man, near an oak that must have been ninety feet tall. Its leaves were tossing hard.

"Naw, the horse is right enough. But we got company." His eyes bulged from under a flat-brimmed riverman's hat. His mouth was missing several teeth, and the muddy beard was slit by a wide pink scar that ran from his left eye down to the rim of his jaw.

"That's no lie," shouted the second man. "We got James Clyman and four mad pilgrims about a half a mile back. Let's go!"

The rain was coming down in sheets now, and my blanket was soaked through. I was thirty yards up the hill from the men when another fork of lightning struck the ridge across the draw. Their horses shied.

"Them pilgrims ain't seen us yet," said the man called Haggard. "But this one has. It's a woman, or else a boy; look there, by the tree." He pointed at me through the gloom.

"Let him go," the second man called back. "We're gonna lose these horses in a minute." The last of the herd was splashing past my lean-to.

Haggard lifted an old flintlock rifle from behind his saddle. "This won't take a minute," he said. "I know just what to do."

A flintlock makes a quick flash before it fires, and instinctively I jerked down when I saw it. I thanked providence and plain luck that he didn't have a newer gun. The rifle ball snicked through a flap in my blanket and into the brush to my left. The scar-faced man swore.

"He's a quick one," he said. "Ducked at the pan flash. Now I got to ride him down."

I backed away on all fours into the brush. I was mad and scared and very wide awake. My knuckles were white around the stock of the rifle.

"No you ain't!" The second rider jammed his horse in the way. "We've lost enough time already. We get these nags over the ridge and we'll have all the start we need. We don't want no dead bodies marking the trail."

I had the rifle, but could I shoot a man? I didn't think so. It went against everything I'd ever been taught.

"I'll catch up with you," Haggard answered. "That boy saw me clear as daybreak, and I sure don't want to leave Clyman with no healthy witness."

I could shoot the horse, maybe, but then the man would be after me on foot. That seemed almost worse. All I wanted was for him to disappear. The rain pounded on my shoulders as another roll of thunder shook the air.

I squatted and flipped the blanket over my head, like a small wet wigwam. Working by feel only, I knocked the powder from the pan and blew it clear. I refilled with dry powder from the horn around my neck, praying that the powder in the barrel was still dry. I snapped down the frizzen and yanked the hammer back. When I looked again, the men were still near the ninety-foot oak.

"All right," the second man was saying. "But if it takes you more than two minutes, I ain't waiting." He turned his horse.

Haggard's mount was dancing sideways, nervous in the storm. I tried to brace my rifle against a sapling with my off hand, but it kept slipping down the wet trunk. I couldn't see my gunsights. My arms were shaking. I knew I shouldn't be shooting at a man, and I also knew this was no way to get it done. I squeezed the trigger.

The ball went wide of Haggard, but it burned a groove in his horse's rump. The animal almost sat down, then came up squealing and left the ground with all four feet. Haggard dropped his rifle in the mud and held on. The horse crow-hopped and spun.

A bright crisp of light went through the rain, spiraled down the trunk of the giant oak, and smashed into the ground. Both horses took off at a dead run.

Eight

JAMES CLYMAN was a man in his fifties—uncommonly old, I thought—with a seamy face and a gravelly Virginia accent. He speared a cornmeal biscuit from where it sizzled in a pan, held it out on the point of his knife, and waggled it.

"Have another biscuit, boy. It isn't much, but you could use the grease."

The rain had let up for the time being, and I could hear the night birds and crickets. Mr. Clyman had made me strip off my clothes, which were now drying on poles by the fire, and had wrapped me tightly in a buffalo robe. But my teeth were still chattering; I didn't know if it was from being wet too long or from the scare I'd had. I felt dazed and jittery at the same time.

Beyond the firelight were the wagons, tents, and gear of an emigrant train. Mr. Clyman had been hired to scout and hunt for them, to guide them out the Oregon Road and over the Rocky Mountains.

I slurped at a tin cup of tea.

"I figure the company could live without that little string of horses," he said. "Lord knows they're driving enough livestock to eat up half the grass in Oregon Territory."

I put down my cup. "My pa says the emigrants leave gear and claptrap all along the trail. He says there will be a line of broken dishes and busted bedsteads from here to California, someday." Mr. Clyman prodded the fire with a stick.

"I've had that same thought myself," he said. "But I guess we have to make a good show of chasing horse thieves, anyway—to earn my keep, if nothing else."

"Where do you think they went?" I asked him.

"Usually when stock disappears around here, you find it later with some of the Kaw tribe. So you end up buying or stealing your own stock back from them, and you risk a haircut in the bargain."

"These men weren't Kaw, and they knew you were following them," I said. "I heard them say your name." He thought a moment while he produced a silver flask from somewhere and poured a little something into his tea.

"That means they know me, somehow," he said. "And shooting at you means they wanted no witnesses—so they think I might know them, too." He reached for my cup.

"No thank you, sir," I said. "I wouldn't care for any of that." Mr. Clyman squinted at me.

"I don't recall asking your preference, boy. Just hold the cup steady; I don't want to waste good rum."

"Sir, the Good Book teaches not to take strong drink. And, besides, my Aunt Judith wouldn't like it." Mr. Clyman paused.

"Is Aunt Judith a Mormon?"

"No sir. Congregational. My pa's French."

"Well, son, Aunt Judith may not have mentioned that our Lord himself turned water into wine."

"Yessir, he did that, but—"

"And the Good Book says, 'Take a little for thy stomach's sake,' doesn't it?"

"Yessir, that's true, but—"

"And it also says, 'All things in moderation.'"

"Yessir, it does."

"Now, you've just been soaked to the skin in a midnight rain, you've been run down by a rustled herd, and you've been shot at by horse thieves in the night. Well, sir, in my book, a little rum in your tea after all that is the absolute gospel sense of moderation. Added to which, you're shaking like a leaf."

"I really couldn't, sir."

Mr. Clyman sighed, and he spoke crossly.

"But most of all, the Good Book says to mind your elders, because it's their job to look out for you. Now, you can call this medicine, if you like, but you drink it down, my friend. I'll explain to your aunt, if it comes to that." He splashed a little rum in my cup and gestured for me to drink.

"Tell me something else," he said gruffly, changing the subject. "This man with the scar—was he a big man or small?"

"Bigger than me," I said. "But not as big as you." Mr. Clyman was four or five inches over six feet—as tall a man as I had ever seen. He was lean and leathery, and his gray hair fell past his shoulders. His eyes were gray, too, as if they had aged along with his hair and the lines in his face. He wore buckskin trousers, and I didn't have to ask if he'd been in the mountains.

"Wearing a riverman's hat, eh? And missing some teeth. Hmm." He thought about that for a while. The rum was warming me from the inside, and I could feel the knots in my stomach loosening one by one. Finally, he shrugged.

"Hmph. No sense guessing; there's a lot of boatmen get into one scrape or another."

"I think the other one called him 'Hacker' or 'Haggard'—one of those names," I offered. Mr. Clyman looked up at me sharply.

"Well, sir," he said. "That would be Thompson Haggard, sure as you're born. And you, my friend, are even luckier to be alive than we knew."

Thompson Haggard, he told me, was known up and down the frontier for a dangerous man—hot-tempered, violent, unpredictable, and mean. He had killed more than one man in fights along the Missouri River. The old free trappers often blamed him for stealing hides, horses, and guns.

But there were other stories about him, too, Mr. Clyman said. Stories of people finding him out of his head, naked, painted in mud and ashes, wandering the river trails weeping and calling aloud in a foreign tongue. He came and went where he wished among the Crow, the Cheyenne, and the Pawnee; they thought he was crazy, and left him alone.

"Last I heard," Mr. Clyman told me, "Haggard was down catching stray Paiutes and selling them to the Mexicans."

"For slaves, you mean?" I asked.

"Yep. You don't hear about it much, but some of the nations down there have been running slaves to Mexico for generations. The Utes have done it. The Kiowas. Some others. So I guess Haggard just reckoned that might be a good living for a while. I hadn't heard he snuck back this direction. Must have come over the trail from Santa Fe."

I shuddered. Mr. Clyman looked over at me.

"There's a lot of badness out there, son, and the Good Book doesn't tell you the half of it."

"Yessir." We were quiet for a minute, and then Mr. Clyman tossed his stick in the fire.

"Now, here's what we'll do." He nodded toward a small lean-to nearby. "That's my rig over there, and it's still pretty dry. I want you to hole up in there tonight, while I see what I can do about your pal Haggard."

I started to say something, but Mr. Clyman held up his hand.

"In the morning—which isn't that far away now—I want you to break it down for me and pack it on that red mule there. See him?"

"Yessir."

"And I bet you know how to diamond-hitch a pack, don't you? So here's our deal: you look after my outfit for me, and you can use it as long as I'm gone."

"Yessir."

"I'll tell the wagon captain not to wait, and I'll meet him by the Kansas River in a few days. You just tag along and be useful. Get next to a man name of Johnny, if you can; he's a good hand." He stopped. "What else?"

I stood up.

"Could I have a little more tea, please, sir?" I asked, holding out my cup. "Without the medicine?"

Nine

My DREAMS were wild—rifle shots booming nearby, Aunt Judith warning and weeping, thunderbolts slicing the sky ragged with scars. I heard a mule braying far away, and then a piercing sound blasted my dreams to cobwebs. Before I was fully awake, I found myself standing, sighting down the flintlock at a man in buckskins. He was backing away with his hands in the air. One of them held a bugle.

"Don't shoot!" He was shouting and starting to giggle at the same time. "Just a little joke, son. I thought you was Clyman. Don't shoot. Don't shoot. Wake up, now, and you get some breeches on." I looked down at my bare legs, and the man dodged behind a tree. As he ran, I could hear him laughing out loud, and he tooted the bugle happily. I laid the rifle aside very carefully and sat down. The mule brayed again.

I had seen wagon trains at Independence with Aunt Judith and Uncle John, but I had never seen one loaded as heavily as this one. These folks were headed for Oregon and California, and they were surely planning not to come back. Personally, I would have left a few of the heavier things with friends or kindred back East. Things like the beds, the sideboards, the tables and chairs, the cast-iron stoves. And the pianos.

But they weren't complaining. They had seen nothing but dirt and heavy lifting for as long as they had been traveling, and still they found a reason to smile, to tell stories, to sing. I wondered if this mud and rain might not dampen their spirits along with their shoes, but I didn't see much sign of it. The rain sure did slow things down, but then driving mules and oxen is not the fastest way to travel, even in the best of weather.

The thing about being wet is that you never quite get used to it; it's never the least bit comfortable. The first morning after I joined the emigrants, it began to drizzle from a wide gray sky, and by the third day we had seen every variety of rain known to humankind. A bank of clouds would steam up from the southwest, and we could see the downpour moving right along with it. The rain would push on overhead and drench us good before passing by. Then we'd see another cloud bank coming. In between, we'd get a mist and fine rain.

Mud was everywhere. Every soul in the group of five hundred was caked and soaked in mud. Black topsoil mud, or gray-green clay mud, or fine brown river mud. From just walking, we had mud to our knees. From working the animals, we had mud to our elbows. Most of us had slipped and sat down in mud, or fallen forward in mud, or been dragged by a team through mud. Women were muddy from the hems of their skirts almost to their waists; muddy older children looked after muddy younger ones, and they all carried something muddy. Men would stop and sit down in mud and empty mud from their boots and rinse them in a muddy stream and pull them back on muddy.

The creeks were high where we forded them, and the banks were greasy with mud. To keep the wheels from sinking, we stuffed branches, logs, driftwood—anything we could drag—into the ruts, or we laid them sideways to the trail. We hitched the teams double so they could pull those heavy wagons through the streams and up the other side. Often a woman would drive the team while two to four men would prize the axles through the mud with beams. A bull whip would pop, or we'd slash at the mules with switches; we'd drag on their lead lines; we'd shove our shoulders into them. And the animals would lunge into the harness, their hooves slipping and gouging. We'd get one rig across, and we'd have to unhitch the second team to drive it back for the next rig in line.

In some places the wheel ruts went knee-deep, and if I looked on up the trail, they were knee-deep as far as I could see through the rain. We might have been better off with skids or runners instead of wheels.

And still it rained. On the fourth day, we were passing through a saddle between two low prairie swells when it started up a steady downpour. Not a thunderstorm, where it's all noise and wind and then it's gone. This was a soaking two-day rain, with drops the size of river pebbles. The soil couldn't take any more, so the water just ran over the ground in every direction. I looked down and saw water washing over the toes of my boots. It was shoe-mouth deep on the women and children. It sloshed into our tents and under the wagons where we slept at night. We went to bed in the rain, and we got up in the rain. We ate wet, walked wet, and thought hard about a life of being wet.

We were the stepchildren of Noah, late for the ark. We were as wet as water could make us.

Ten

"**H**ow come your Aunt Judith don't like your daddy?" the man with the bugle asked me. We sat under a wide canvas in a light drizzle; our campfire hissed against the wet wood. His name was Pickett. His face was narrow, his hair plastered to both sides by the rain. He came from Illinois or Michigan, I think, and he had been to California a couple of times. He was looking for a group to lead out there again, and said he knew a cutoff to make the trip shorter. He was the kind of man that my pa said was always looking for some quick money, and usually at the expense of other folks. He was friendly, but he talked all the time.

"Maybe Aunt Judith just can't abide the Frenchies, eh? Maybe she don't approve of Catholics," Pickett said.

"I don't know," I answered. "Since my mother died, Aunt Judith doesn't like much of anyone." I was running a patch down my rifle barrel, trying to get it dry and trying to look too busy to talk.

The truth is that my aunt didn't like Pa, or his free-trapper friends, or rivermen, or soldiers, or any other man who spent months away from farm and family. Farm and family—that's what Aunt Judith said was the only way to settle a country.

"What did your ma die of?" Pickett asked. He was full of questions.

"Died in childbed ten years ago, they told me," I said. "I was four, and I don't recall much about it." I didn't look up as I rammed another patch down.

"Bet your pa was gone, wasn't he? Aunt Judith didn't like that, neither." Pickett made a clucking sound.

I drew out the dry patch on the end of the ramrod and studied it, thinking about Etienne, my pa. I could see his broad hands and his forearms, ropy with muscle. His face was square, open, and friendly, and his eyes seemed to watch everything, all the time. I could hear his laugh and the music of the French in his voice.

"That was when we lived in St. Charles, and he was up the Missouri," I told Pickett. Pa worked the keelboats, and then the steamboats, before he went to the Rockies. I didn't remember much about that time, except his wild stories, the sheer strength of his arms, and the joy that I could see in my mother when he came home. She and I both loved him with whole hearts.

"That's the trouble with them Frenchies," Pickett said. "They're handsome and jolly, but you can't no-wise depend on them."

Pa told me later that he had meant to be home when the baby was born, but my mother had an early labor.

I remember the birth myself; that is, I remember the screaming. It was only a kind of shouting at first, and lots of moaning. I remember Aunt Judith saying crossly that the baby was breech and wouldn't turn; I didn't know what she meant, and she sent me away. But the shouting bothered me, and then it turned to screaming. I covered my ears and hummed to myself to drown out the noise; I cried a little, and I hid under the table. After a while, the screaming went hoarse, and then it went away, and Aunt Judith sat alone at the table crying and crying. She wouldn't let me see my mother.

A week later, Pa was home. There was no joy in him this time, but he held me in his strong arms and whispered French words over and over into my hair.

"*Tais-toi,* my son. Be still. *Maman* is with the saints and angels now. *Tais-toi.*"

I remember holding his big hat, flopping it onto my head while we stood looking at the mound of fresh earth and green grass where they had put my mother. He carried me everywhere for a week.

Then he was gone again, this time to the Rockies, and Aunt Judith settled into her gray granite face. She and Uncle John and I moved from St. Charles up to Caldwell, and they started the farm. Pa came back for a month every summer, bringing bundled beaver pelts for Uncle John to sell in St. Louis, new moccasins for me, and usually a buffalo robe.

And stories, always stories. He spent hours telling me tales of grizzly bears and buffalo, of fights among the trappers at rendezvous, of friends he had made among the Utes and the Cheyennes and the Shoshones. When I was nine, he gave me his flintlock rifle and taught me how to shoot it and care for it. Each time he came to visit, Aunt Judith was colder than the time before.

But then the fur trade disappeared. Pa said it was because the rich men back East wanted silk hats now. He said the beavers were getting scarce anyway, so it was a good thing to stop trapping them. He hoped the French and English and Americans would get out of the mountains and go back to the cities in the East.

I wondered if that meant he would stay home for good now. But he said no; he had to get back and look after his cache and a few other things. He said he might work as a guide for some of the emigrants that were starting to cross the mountains for Oregon. Or he might be an interpreter between the whites and the Indians. He wouldn't look at me when he said these things. He seemed restless.

Last year, when I was thirteen, I wanted to go with him.

"Not yet, *mon ami*," Pa said. "You help Aunt Judith and you make the education. Every day you read, you write. I coming back for you two years' time, you see? Then you are ready." He squeezed my shoulders in his large hands and kissed me good night. In the morning, he was gone.

Pickett was making shadows in the firelight with his fingers. A rabbit. A wolf. A wolf eating a rabbit.

"So you really think you can find him, boy?" he wanted to know.

"I have to find him," I said.

Pickett snorted. "Sure, and I have to marry me a rich Mexican widow." He made two wolf shadows, howling with their chins in the air.

"No," I said firmly. "Something's happened to him. I'm sure of it."

Pickett looked at me sideways, and then he stared off into the night and the rain.

"I don't doubt it, son," he said. "Don't doubt it one bit."

Eleven

THE OTHER THING about being wet is that you
never get a good chance to wash your clothes. The constant mud keeps you from getting clean, and the constant
rain keeps you from getting dry. So, when one day dawned
clear and bright, I crossed myself the way my "Frenchie"
pa always did to steady his luck. The luck held. We stopped
for our nooning beside a wide oxbow not far from where a
sizable stream emptied into the Kansas River.

Cut off when the main channel had moved years ago,
the oxbow made a long, quiet curve lined with cottonwoods and willow trees so wide I couldn't get my arms
halfway around any of them. The water was high from all
the rain, and there was almost no current. It swung in wide
eddies near hollows in the bank, and slowed into deep
pools sheltered under the trees. The emigrants made the
most of the moment. Men and boys tipped over trunks to
drain them and laid out everything wet to dry in the sun.
Women carried clothes down to the water for washing and
hung them on the lower branches. Some of the children

cut poles for fishing, while others kept busy skimming stones across the surface.

I was desperate to wash my own clothes. They were near to worn out when I started this walk, and the wet weather hadn't improved them a bit. Mud had made a crust to the knees of my trousers, and more mud had dried in a stiff circle from the back of one thigh, across my rear, and down the other side. My shirt was no better.

I found a cove well away from the women and children where the stream made a quiet pool under the protection of three low-slung willow trees. I struggled out of my stiff clothes and set to work. Wading out into the stream, I ducked the trousers under the surface and scrubbed their legs together roughly. I rinsed them. I wrung them out. I pounded them against tree trunks. I scrubbed and rinsed and scrubbed again. When the trousers began to look better, I set to work on my shirt and my drawers. I was so pleased with the job when I finally draped them all on a low limb that I decided to relax and have a swim.

There's nothing like swimming naked in a cool stream on a hot day for making you feel clean and lively. I dove to the bottom and brought up stones as large as I could carry. I lay on my back and drifted a bit, then turned over and thrashed my way back to the cove. I played. I rested. I let the slow current soak away all the crust and grit of the trail. Finally, I stepped out onto the bank. I loved the feel of my skin puckering slightly in the breeze; I held out my arms and turned round and round, feeling silly and glad no one could see me.

My clothes looked passably dry as I stepped over to drag them from their limb. But, reaching upward, I noticed something in the tree that I had missed before. It was a bare foot. Attached to a leg. A bare leg. And somewhere above the leg was a dark face frowning fiercely and blushing in a cloud of brown curls. A girl. My foot slipped and I fell backward like a log into the water.

"What do you think you're doing?" I demanded, hunched down in the stream to cover myself. I was too angry even to blush.

"Well, I was *doing* just fine," she snapped, "until certain people tramped in and interrupted me. You're not the only one who needs to wash clothes, you know." She was standing on the limb, but she was mostly hidden by the trunk of the tree.

"You've been up there the whole time, just . . . just spying on me!"

"Where was I supposed to go, Master Washerwoman? *My* clothes are in that tree over there, as any fool can see."

I looked where she was pointing. Sure enough, neatly arranged along a low limb were a muslin skirt, an apron, a chemise, and, well, some other things that girls wear. She was just as naked as I was. Now I could feel myself blushing.

"Well, you just gather them up and get out of here," I said.

"I was here first; you get *your* things and leave." The angry brown eyes flashed.

"Not a chance."

I stayed hunched up in the water; she stayed in the tree. We weren't getting anywhere. Finally, I decided to bluff.

"All right," I said. "If I leave first, I'll just take your things with me." I started to stand up.

"You touch my clothes," she threatened, "and I'll cut your pitiful trousers to ribbons." She reached my trousers with two of her toes and tugged them closer. I held up my hand.

"Hold on," I said, squatting back down in the water.

"Now, you listen here," she commanded. "You turn right around and swim back out where you were. You keep your eyes to yourself, and I'll be gone in five minutes." I didn't like taking orders from a girl, but I could see the sense in what she said. I moved carefully out toward the deeper water.

"Well, you keep *your* eyes to yourself," I said. She snorted.

I drifted a short way with the current, past the tree where her clean clothes hung. I know I should have left well enough alone, but her tone of voice irked me. As I passed her things, it seemed such a good idea just to splash them a little. Just a little ball of wet river sand on her fresh apron—since she showed so much grit. Yes.

"I don't think you got them quite clean!" I called out. She muttered something I didn't hear.

The sun was warm, and the day was lazy. I enjoyed the water and daydreamed a bit while I waited for her to finish.

It was going to feel so good to step into clean clothes for the first time in so long; even if it rained tomorrow, wearing dry trousers today made it all worthwhile.

Her voice came from much too close. I looked up, startled, and there she stood on the riverbank, practically beside me. She was dressed, and smiling. I could see the smear on her apron where my little mudball had struck. And my clothes were wadded in her right hand.

"Thank you for pointing out the fresh mud on my apron," she said, too sweetly. "Seeing how important cleanliness is to you, I felt sure you'd want to give your things just one more wash before you go." She smiled. A fierce smile.

"Wait a minute," I said. She held up her hand.

"Oh, I'm very sorry," she said. "But I must get back to the camp. No time for chatter. You see, the wagons are starting to move out." She smiled again and launched my clean, dry clothes in a high arc through the sky. "See you soon!" she called.

My clothes plopped into the river behind me.

Twelve

Two days of full sun raised the spirits of everyone in the caravan. The ground wasn't much drier, but at least we got muddy only from our feet upward, instead of from all directions at once. Travel was still very slow—maybe eight miles of wet slogging every day. We had left Westport ten days before, and we were only now coming up on the Kansas River crossing. The older men were concerned about floods. All the streams we crossed drained into the Kansas, which drained into the Missouri, which ran more or less east from here till it found the Mississippi. If the rainy season didn't slack off, the whole country was going to be under water from here to St. Louis.

Leading Mr. Clyman's pack mule, I kept out to one side of the main body of the wagons. It wasn't difficult going; the ground was soggy, but at least the mule and I could avoid the sloppiness of the wagon road. I let my mind wander ahead. I could feel myself growing eager to move, eager to see my pa. And at the same time, the distance that lay before me was so long, and Aunt Judith's worry hung in the back of my mind like a little dark cloud. *You have no idea what the world is like.*

We had been traveling westward along the old Santa Fe Trail. In my mind, I could see it as my pa had described it, stretching out for five hundred miles across the Southern Plains, growing drier and drier until rain and rivers were only memories evaporating in the past. Crossing the Cimarron region, where the pack trains traveled for ten days without hope of a watering hole, the trail dropped into New Mexico. And then the mountains rose like a mirage from the desert, Pa said. Finally the road found the old town of Santa Fe. My pa had been there, and he said it was a town with an ancient feel. It was older than St. Louis, even older than Boston or Plymouth. Mexicans, Americans, and Indians met each other there for barter and resupply. Trade goods like woven cloth, tools, beads, tin pans, and guns came from Mexico and California. Utes and Apaches, Navajos and Comanches brought furs and horses from all around. French, English, and American trappers came down from the north, Mexicans arrived from the south, and lately, American settlers came from back east. The town of Santa Fe absorbed them all. I shook my head. It would take me a hundred years of walking to see all I wanted to see.

At the point where the Oregon Trail left the Santa Fe Trail and headed northwest, someone had put up a sign. It was the plainest weather-beaten board nailed to a pole, and "Road to Oregon" was what it said. To me it seemed the edge of the world. On that wide prairie, where everything was new and strange, I thought a sign should point to more than these sorry wheel ruts in the mud.

A man on an old farm horse rode up beside me and stopped.

"You can read writing, my friend?" he asked in a quiet voice.

"Yessir," I answered. "Road to Oregon."

"Huh." He looked ahead over the prairie swells to the empty skyline in the west, then north to a clutch of cottonwoods gathered along a stream maybe a mile away. Halfway between, a pair of hawks circled, studying something far below them on the ground. He took it all in and sighed, and then he looked back at the sign.

"Road to Oregon," he repeated. "A small sign for a big dream. Why not Road to China? Road to the Moon?" He pushed back his hat, and a smile opened slowly across his warm brown face. "Why not Road to Freedom?"

PART TWO

Road to Oregon

One

EVERYONE CALLED HIM "Johnny" except his mother.

About seventy-five years ago, while the Boston colonists were calling for independence from the English, his grandmother's entire village in West Africa was taken captive by Italian slave traders. The villagers were shipped to the New World, and Johnny's mother was born in Jamaica. She was called Luisa by the slavers, and when she was twelve she was sold for a house servant to an English plantation. At fifteen, Luisa was sold to a wealthy man in Virginia, and then to one of the tenant farms that belonged to General George Washington. She spoke creole English and some Italian, and she named her son Gianni.

Mr. Clyman's family were farmers on the same land, and when General Washington died, Mr. Clyman's father paid for Luisa's freedom and her son's. She and young Johnny moved with the Clymans to Ohio in 1811. Luisa became a midwife and something of a prophet among the black people of southern Ohio. She saw visions, and would sometimes predict the future. Before she died in 1840, she told Johnny he would live to kill buffalo, marry an Indian, and see the mountains in snow. Johnny laughed when he told me this.

"Not a bad fortune, eh, my friend?"

Johnny had been born in Virginia, but he spoke Luisa's English of the Islands. His face was round, his skin a deep coffee color. There were three short parallel scars scored on each cheek, and his eyes seemed to keep laughing even when he was not. He was small, not much larger than me, but I never saw a man handle a horse smoother than he did. I had the sense that in his small bones he was uncommonly strong, limber, and quick. He was quiet, too, unlike Pickett, and I spent most days walking beside him as he rode, while I led Mr. Clyman's red mule. I wondered so many things about him. What did his scars mean? What brought him to the West? Was he looking for someone, like I was?

"Ohio's a free state," I said one afternoon. "Why did you leave there?"

Johnny smiled.

"Ohio a free state, my friend," he said, "but no state know what to do with a free black man."

"Where is your father?" I asked him.

He had a way of pulling his eyebrows together while his mouth smiled—a look that said he couldn't believe how stupid I was.

"Sorry," I mumbled.

"I think about these buffaloes out West," he said. "I think these buffaloes show me more freedom than Ohio. Maybe a place for me out there."

We camped in a stand of timber near a stream that fed the Kansas River. Johnny shot a rabbit, and we were roasting him over a small fire when Pickett came by to chaff me about drying out my old Bible. I had it propped against a flat stone and I was opening some wet pages one by one toward the fire.

"You mind what you're doing, boy," he said to me. "The Word of the Lord is supposed to be a flame; it ain't supposed to go up in flames. Haw haw haw." Johnny's eyes went from me to Pickett and back.

"Yessir," I said. "Aunt Judith would roast me like this rabbit if that happened." Pickett had taken too many cracks at me for reading, and I wanted to move him on to another subject. Johnny did it for me.

"Pickett like to keep the Word wet; he burn himself on it one time."

Pickett snickered high in his nose.

"Do you think Mr. Clyman got those horses yet?" I asked.

"Don't ask me," Pickett replied. "Johnny here is the one with second sight."

Johnny raised one eyebrow as he turned the rabbit over the fire. "Mr. Clyman be back soon, but I think he don't get many horses."

"Do you really have second sight?" I asked. "Like your mother?"

"Sure he does," Pickett said with a straight face. "Johnny sees two of everything!" That got him snickering again, till I thought he was going to sneeze his hat off.

Johnny laughed, too, and then he did an amazing thing. He reached over to where Pickett squatted beside him, and he pulled a roasted rabbit leg from Pickett's ear. Pickett shrieked with laughter as Johnny sank his teeth into the dark meat.

"Ain't that something?" Pickett giggled. "He does magic tricks like that all the time. And he'll read your mind, too. He can do it."

"I give up reading Pickett's mind anymore." Johnny grinned. "They nothing there I want to know." This set Pickett sneezing again. Johnny held out the other hind leg to me, made it disappear, then plucked it out of the air between us. He handed it over, laughing quietly.

"You, my young Daniel in the lion's den, you cite us up some Good Book text for dinner grace."

"I don't know . . ." I said.

"Yes, yes, you know. We need some Good Book like the auntie teach you."

Pickett agreed.

"That's right, Frenchie. Give us a little scripture blessing here."

"Suffer the children to come unto me," I quoted, hoping this would make them leave me alone.

"Ah, children," Johnny said, looking close at me. He quoted something from Jeremiah. "Rachel, she weep her children, for they no more."

Pickett clapped and snorted.

"It's a hard life for the young 'uns." He chuckled.

But I hadn't been raised by Aunt Judith for nothing. I came back with Proverbs. I stood up.

"Her children will rise up and call her blessed," I recited. Johnny stood up, too, and the look in his eye was a dare. He quoted a bloody passage from Matthew.

"Herod send and slay all boy children two year and younger."

I didn't like the direction he was taking this, but I still thought I could turn him. The book of Genesis.

"The Lord said to Abraham, now count the stars—so many shall your children be."

Never taking his eyes from mine, Johnny reached into the dark and a knife appeared in his fist. His voice was sharp and hot.

"Abraham stretch out his hand and take the knife to slay his son." He sliced the air between us three times. I swallowed. Hard. Pickett was quiet.

"And the Lord provided a ram in a thicket," I whispered.

Johnny made the knife go away, and then he put his face close to mine.

"Now I reading your mind, Daniel the walker," he whispered. "And it say, 'Father, my father, why you have forsaken me?'"

Two

THE BLUE SKY didn't last. After one morning's battering drizzle, we were soaked again in every part and particular. Falling asleep was a matter of getting warm enough for it, not of getting comfortable. All night, I could hear children coughing and parents bickering.

Mr. Clyman came back with eight of the stolen horses, which he hobbled and turned out into a sodden meadow where most of the stock was kept. Leading his own horse, he splashed up to Johnny and me just after dark on the night before we crossed the river. Johnny handed him a cup of hot tea and began unsaddling the horse without a single word.

"Thank you, my friend," Mr. Clyman sighed. "Just what the doctor ordered."

It was as if Johnny had known exactly when to expect him; he poured the tea in a tin cup right as I was wondering who that could be sloshing around in the dark. And Mr. Clyman wasn't surprised. He winked at me.

"Johnny and me go way back" was all he said. He sat against a tree and was asleep before he finished his cup.

It took two full days for all the wagons to cross the Kansas River. The rain had filled the river, so that all the low ground along it was flooded. We waded knee-deep in water getting to the so-called bank of the river, where we could reach the ferry. The first wagons across sloshed up the other side in search of high ground, and they kept on going. It was eight days before the whole group was together again.

We traveled along prairie ridges that ran between the streams, making our way generally north and west, hoping someday to find the Platte River. Most days, it seemed two lifetimes ahead of us. We rafted or used bull boats to cross the rivers we couldn't ford, and the men in the caravan spent a good deal of time disputing where to cross and whether we should have come this way at all.

All the streams were running high. The prairie was so soaked in places that it would not hold the weight of a full-grown man. We kept to the ridges and rocky stretches, and made less than ten miles a day most of the time. Once, it rained for eighty hours straight. And whenever the rain eased off, the mosquitoes were after us in hungry clouds.

Some of the children had caught the croup, some were colicky. All of us had colds. There were some folks with consumption who were heading west for their health. This weather was not doing them any good, though no one had died yet. It wasn't any better for the animals. Oxen, horses, and mules suffered from the fouls in their hooves, in their mouths, and in their bowels. Mr. Clyman said these emigrants, who at first had all been laughing and hopeful, "now showed dejection in every face."

When we crossed deep water, everything had to be unloaded from the wagons and loaded onto rafts or bull boats. But rafts and round-bottom boats are hard to steer, and from time to time one would get swamped or speared on a snag, and half a family's food and dry goods would end up in the drink. By the time we all got across, the riverbanks would be decorated with broken crockery, broken bottles, sodden scraps of food, clothing trampled and torn, gunny sacks soiled and sad-looking—loose bits of lives swept away on the current and spilled along both shores.

At the base of especially steep hills, or on the drier side of especially muddy patches, we saw the discarded household goods of travelers who had passed this way before. Rotting bedsteads and hutches, broken-down sideboards and secretaries huddled in the rain as if they were looking for a ride west. We passed them by, and left some of our own heavier baggage to keep them company.

There were some who wanted to turn back, and I have to say I gave it some thought myself. Fort Bridger seemed so far, and in the mist and rain we seemed to be walking in place, slogging through the same puddle again and again, not moving forward at all. If we didn't move faster, I would never reach my pa in time. *Don't think how far,* I told myself. Putting one foot in front of the other was all I dared to think about. Because Pickett was right—how would I find Etienne, if and when I did get there?

We trudged onward.

Somehow, day by day, the rain seemed lighter, like we were traveling slowly out from under a great roof of weather. Soon the creeks were only high, instead of flooding, and the rain was no longer constant. On the Fourth of July, the sun rose red and giant through a mist without rain, and the men on guard fired off their guns to greet it.

We were overtaken by a smaller wagon train, mostly composed of men with lung sickness and consumption. Some promoter had promised that the dry air in California would cure them, and had got a bunch of them together to make the trip. Mr. Clyman told me some had died along the way, and others looked like they were not long for this world.

But they brought news of the settlements back in Missouri. Even if our weather was lighter now, the flooding back downstream was fierce. Whole towns and villages were swamped. Fences, barns, and farmhouses had been simply washed away; some wagons were swept downriver without a trace. Cholera was in epidemic, and sickness of every kind was claiming poor souls from Independence to St. Louis.

I thought of Aunt Judith and Uncle John. Our farm was safe on its hilltop, though the road to Caldwell might wash out in places. But if there were sick folk nearby to be tended, Aunt Judith would surely be calling on them. I said a blessing for her health, and ended it with *"merci, bon Dieu,"* the way Pa always did, though I knew she wouldn't have liked it.

Whatever happened, these spring rains of 1844 would be remembered for years.

Three

During the winter after my pa went to the Rockies for the first time, I came down with fever. Aunt Judith said it was an infection in my ears, and not the scarlet fever like the doctor said. She dribbled warm sweet oil in my ears and heated a small bag of salt to lay my head on. She sat up nights with me until the fever broke. It was during this time that I began to have dreams.

Some people have different dreams every night, but I had only two dreams, over and over.

In the first dream, I could see the devil at the sickroom door. The devil himself. He was small, like an old woman. He smelled of blood and black powder, and he wore a stovepipe hat made from beaver felt. He looked a little sweaty. The devil leaned in the doorway and smiled, and he spoke rapidly in a light and friendly voice.

"I can make you well, you know."

"You can?"

"Certainly, of course, why not? Do it all the time for boys your age." He smiled again. "And all you have to do is . . . take up your bed and walk!"

I didn't think it was right for the devil to be quoting scripture, though the scripture says he'll do that sometimes. I struggled to sit up, but I was too weak with fever.

Suddenly his clammy face was leaning close and dripping sweat into my eyes, and he sat down on my chest.

"Can't move? But you must. Get up, get up, get up!" he urged. "Take up your bed." But I couldn't move.

"You're hurting me," I groaned. His weight was getting heavier and heavier, till I began to gasp.

"Not hurting. Not I. Not at all, scripture boy," he whispered. "If you can't do it, your faith is too weak. You don't deserve to live. Oh, ye of little faith. Little faith." He pressed his hot hands down over my mouth and squeezed, while he pushed down on my chest with all his weight. I was paralyzed, too weak to make a sound.

Then Aunt Judith was there, wiping my face with a cool rag.

"Daniel. Wake up, honey. Wake up." She looked down at me in the candlelight with her eyebrows drawn together and a strand of hair falling down.

"You stopped breathing again, Daniel," she said. "I do wish you'd quit doing that." Her hand on my face was cool, and I thought she was my mother back from the grave. We watched each other for a long time, until I fell asleep again.

In the morning there was blood on the pillow, and my fever had broken.

That was the spring we moved from St. Charles to Caldwell. Pa had said he would be home in June, and after we moved I was worried that he might have trouble finding us. Maybe that was why I started having the second dream.

In this dream, I was trying to cross a wagon road in the dark. I stepped up to the road, but suddenly wagons were passing in front of me, cutting me off. They were moving slowly in a line, the oxen silent and the drivers staring straight ahead like dead men. One of the wagons slowly caught fire, then another. I moved closer to watch, while the burning wagons passed slowly by and the fire gathered them under its orange wings. Then I saw my pa.

He was on the other side of the road, looking straight at me through the flames. His face was smeared with soot, and there was blood on his sleeve.

"Daniel," he called. "*Bouge pas.* Don't move from there. I coming to find you very quick. Stay back from the fire."

When I told Aunt Judith about this dream, she waved me away.

"Fretting over dreams is pure idleness. Go and fetch the kindling now."

I had that dream three more times, and then it went away. When Pa arrived late in June, his hair was short. He said it had been singed in a fire and he'd cut it off. There were burn blisters on the back of one hand, and he wore a bulky bandage above his right elbow.

Four

THINKING about the dreams made me restless somehow, and impatient with how slowly our caravan moved. Even though we had been picking up speed, I wished I had gone ahead with the other wagon train. They were maybe two days ahead of us by now. For a moment, I wondered if I could catch them; then I gave up that idea. We were into Pawnee country now, and although they left wagon trains alone, especially big ones like this, they were always happy to pick up solitary travelers or stray livestock. Still, I told myself, Pa traveled alone sometimes. Mr. Clyman had done it, too, and there were stories of other free trappers who did.

The evening was cool and dry, with a breeze from the north. In fact, the wind had been blowing steadier the farther we got out onto the plains. It was a relief to be done with the rain, but the wind was strange to me. It kept everything constantly flapping, and put a good bit of dust in the air.

We made camp in a stand of timber near the south bank of the Platte. I wished we were farther along, but, still, out here, where the ground was drier, we were making better time than before. We had come some distance along what Mr. Clyman called the Old Platte Road. This was the route he and other trappers often took to the mountains twenty years ago, though now it was considered just a part of the Oregon Trail.

The wagons were set in several rough squares, keeping the livestock more or less penned in the centers. I picketed Mr. Clyman's mule near our lean-to, and then wandered a short way through the trees. The stars were just beginning to appear in the sky on maybe the pleasantest evening in six weeks. I leaned against a cottonwood and took a deep breath.

"I have to tell you, that shirt and those trousers are very nearly indecent."

I jumped at the sound of her voice, and grabbed hold of the tree to keep my balance.

"Did I startle you again?"

She was seated on a fallen log a few yards away with her back against a tree. She wore the same neat apron I had seen before over a dark-blue skirt. Her curly hair was dark and shorter than I remembered, and she had a spray of freckles across her nose. She looked exactly like the most prissy girls I knew back in Caldwell, Missouri.

"Yes, you startled me," I snapped. "I don't like people sneaking up on me like that." Girls always made me feel stupid, and the girls around Caldwell were nowhere near as forward as this one. I did like her smile, though, in spite of myself.

"I didn't sneak, you great galoot. You nearly tripped over me." Then she was all business. "Truly, what will you give me to make you a new set of clothes? I have cotton broadcloth and muslin, and I can have them done in four days. I've done it for your Mr. Clyman. Or I can make the trousers out of buckskin, if you like, but that will take longer." She spoke rapidly and looked me over like you might judge a horse. "Either way, you need new clothes bad."

"I don't have anything to trade you," I said. "And . . . and you shouldn't speak so forward to people you don't even know." Why did talking to her make me blush and say foolish things?

Her face went blank for an instant, and then she laughed five light descending notes: *so-fa-mi-re-do*.

"How can you say I don't know you?" she teased. "I had to watch you skinny-dipping for almost half an hour." She laughed again. "Why, I'm only fourteen, but if my father were alive, he'd have made you marry me three Sundays back."

"Blush" is not the word; I was red from my face to my knees. I made a sharp left turn and escaped through the underbrush.

"What about your clothes?" she called. "You think about it!"

I kept on going, crashing through the brush like an ox in a panic, till I came back around to the red mule and our lean-to. I gathered up the flintlock, pouch, and powder horn, tied the blanket to my pack, and shouldered it. I filled my pockets with jerked venison and headed back into the brush.

The moon gave plenty of light for me to follow wagon tracks. I figured I would trot as far as I could tonight, sleep all day, and maybe catch the sick wagons in two more nights of running.

I came past the place where she had been, and didn't stop. She was walking away now, which suited me fine. I paused to let my eyes get accustomed to the growing darkness, and then I found a little game trail that would take me past the wagons. It was good to be on the move again.

I came around a bend in the trail, and something dark swung toward me through the twilight. I shouted once before the world went black.

Five

I COULD FEEL MYSELF falling for a long time, but when I hit the ground, it didn't hurt at all. Nothing hurt. On the other hand, I knew that couldn't be right. Something had happened that scared me, and my body wanted to run away as fast as I could make it go.

From far away a face came into view. Everything around the face was blurry, a tangle of leaves and twigs and fur, but the face was clear.

And ugly. Gray-blotched whiskers and ragged teeth in the front of the mouth. There was a knife scar that ran from the left temple to the rim of the jaw. It was Haggard. I yelled, and someone hit me again, right below my left eye. This time it hurt bad, but it didn't knock me out.

"One more sound and I'll slit your throat, white boy," Haggard murmured. To his right was the man who had hit me. He was an Indian man with a knobby chin and a tattoo on his left cheek. He wore buckskins like Haggard did, and there were two feathers tied in his hair. I thought he might be a Pawnee.

"You don't make sense, boy." Haggard chuckled. "One minute you're talking to a pretty little miss, and the next minute you're running like a scared colt." He smirked. "What'd she do—ask you to marry her?"

I know it was stupid, but that made me mad. I spat at him.

"And what are *you* doing, Haggard? Stealing horses again?"

He pulled me halfway off the ground by my shirt front.

"Where'd you hear that name, boy? Huh? You answer sharp and don't make me ask again." The veins in his face were bulging, and his eyes twitched wildly.

"I heard you talking to your partner in the rain," I whispered angrily. "Don't you remember? I shot your stupid horse!"

He froze. Then he dropped my shirt and sat back on his heels, laughing and laughing silently through his ragged teeth.

"So that was you," he said. He was almost in tears from laughing. This man was crazy.

"You shot my stupid horse, haw haw haw. That you did, boy. And my stupid horse nearly broke my stupid back. I never had a ride like that in my entire stupid life."

I sat very still. He put his hand to his forehead and laughed some more. Then he slapped my face. My face had been aching already, and now I could feel it starting to swell up.

Still laughing, he said something to his friend and waved him away. The man got up and slipped off into the darkness. I could hear horses moving a few yards away. Then Haggard wasn't laughing anymore. He grabbed my shirt again and yanked me to my feet.

I panicked. Instead of standing up with him, I twisted his wrist and kicked wildly upward. He wasn't expecting it, and my foot caught him in the secrets. He gasped and staggered. I rolled to one side, but my ankles got caught with his, tripping him. He went down sideways in the brambles while I scrambled away on all fours.

Now my legs were working fine, and I pumped them as fast as I could through the undergrowth. I jumped a fallen log, dodged around a tree, and plowed through the clutching branches. I stole a quick glance behind me as I ran. Haggard was coming, and he was a far better runner than I was. He moved like smoke on a breeze—silently gliding past and over and around everything in his path. And he was gaining on me, drawing his knife as he came.

A tree. A log. A swinging branch. I dashed through a shallow stream and fell as I climbed up the far bank. My lungs ached from running. I staggered up, and Haggard was on me like a big cat. He caught my hair in one hand and yanked my head back till I thought my neck would pop. The blade of his knife was an inch away from my eyes, making me stand very still.

"Thompson Haggard!" It was Mr. Clyman's voice. "Haggard, you let the boy go, and you let him go right now."

I rolled my eyes toward the sound of his voice, and I could see Mr. Clyman standing with his rifle to his shoulder, some twenty yards away. To his left, I could see Johnny sliding sideways through the dark trees, coming to a stop much closer to Haggard and me. Haggard was watching Mr. Clyman, and I didn't think he saw Johnny moving in. Mr. Clyman kept talking.

"I can take your head off, Haggard, and never scratch the boy," he said evenly. "You know I can do it."

Haggard shifted on his feet. He was still breathing hard from the run.

"I don't know, Clements," he panted. "It's been a few years; maybe your aim is shaky in your old age."

"Could be," agreed Mr. Clyman. "Shall we see if you're right? Either way, I'm tired of waiting." The gun barrel never wavered. Haggard moved the knife blade very slowly upward. It was above my eyebrows now.

"Tell you what let's do," he offered. "Let's see if you can take off my head quicker than I can take off this boy's scalp. How about that, Clements?" His laugh was crazy, but his hand in my hair never let up. He was stronger than two of me and he knew it. He rested the blade against my forehead and gently pressed the cold razor edge of it in. I felt the blood begin to run.

"Well, I don't know," said Mr. Clyman. "That sounds fair. What do you think, Johnny?"

I was right: Haggard hadn't seen Johnny. He jerked his head sharply left and right, searching. His indecision gave me a chance, and I slipped both hands inside his wrist, pushing the knife away from my face. As I did this, Johnny made a small movement, and his own knife appeared in Haggard's shoulder. Haggard yelped and let go of my hair. I dropped to the ground. The gun went off.

Haggard bunched himself and rolled down the bank to the water. We heard him jump the stream, laughing and swearing as he ran. A minute later, the sound of horse hooves came to us through the darkness.

"Well," Mr. Clyman said to Johnny, "I guess I missed."

I knelt in the weeds and threw up.

Six

MR. CLYMAN handed Johnny a long strip of
muslin.

"You think this will do?" he asked.

"Yessir," Johnny said, holding it up. "It look pretty clean;
plenty long enough." He grinned at me.

"You be having a nice come-to-manhood scar, just like
me, you think?" I studied the parallel lines on his cheek-
bones. They had seemed strange to me before—even a little
frightening—but now they were a comfort.

"Did you throw up when you got them?" I wanted to
know.

"Oh yes, my friend," he laughed. "I throw up, I throw
down, I throw every way. Throw up is nothing: body telling
you about danger."

Mr. Clyman spoke up. "What I want to know is where
in the devil you thought you were going. You had your gun
and pack, and you were heading out."

"I don't know."

"You don't know?" He squatted right in front of me, and he was not pleased. "Boy, that is the gospel truth. Because you have no earthly idea where you are, where you're headed, nor what lies between here and there."

"Fort Bridger!" I snapped. "I was going to Fort Bridger. These overloaded city wagons just poke along like sleepwalkers."

Mr. Clyman spat and sat back on a flat stone.

"You may not like the pace, little pilgrim, but this poky bunch of city people is all that's going to keep you alive out here. Try that again and you won't find your pa in this life, that's sure."

"I could have made it," I said, though I knew I was being foolish. Johnny snorted.

"You barely make it past the horses. If Scarface don't grab you, what you going to do about the Pawnee? The coyotes? Or the wolves?"

He wrapped the muslin twice around my head and tied it tightly above my ear. Mr. Clyman judged it critically, then he grinned.

"Looks about right, Johnny. With that headband, he'd make a mighty fine Shawnee husband back East—if he weren't so ugly."

I groaned.

"Don't talk about marriage," I said. "That's what got me into this in the first place."

"Oh yes, Miss Rosalie." Johnny winked. "Very smart wife. You be nice, she maybe save your life again sometime."

"She's *not* my wife!"

Mr. Clyman laughed out loud.

"You sure have a thin skin for such a fighter, boy," he said. "And she did save your life. At least your scalp, which is pretty much the same thing."

"What do you mean?" I asked.

"She hear you cry out and she come running," Johnny explained. "Very simple." He chuckled.

"That's right," Mr. Clyman added. "She ran up saying, 'Two men are killing that boy with the dreadful clothes!'" They had a good laugh about that.

"My clothes are fine," I said, scowling.

"Sure, sure." Johnny grinned. "Pint of blood down the front make you very colorful."

They told me her name was Rosalie McCulloch. She was an orphan, traveling as a house servant with one of the families in the caravan. But they said the family found her too independent, and were set on dismissing her when they got to Oregon. Mr. Clyman and Johnny didn't know much more about her, like what became of her parents. They knew she'd been at a boarding school in St. Louis, and they knew she could sew. She took in mending from all the men in our caravan without families. Mr. Clyman himself had paid her to make him new wool trousers for the winter. Pickett had given her a pair of tanned deer hides to make into a war shirt for him.

"Not sure she can make a war shirt," Mr. Clyman said.

"It's a medicine shirt, really. Usually takes an Indian woman to make one proper."

"Oh yes, it's very difficult," said a cheerful voice. "I can't decide which is going to be harder for me: wasting buck-skin on all that silly fringe, or just getting the neck hole big enough for an old trapper's fat head." For the third time she had startled me—only this time I had to laugh with her as she moved briskly into the firelight. Mr. Clyman's jaw dropped open, and Johnny sat down hard, rubbing a smile away with the back of his hand. Rosalie stepped over to inspect my bandage.

"Look what you've done, Johnny," she said. "You've made my true love look like a refugee from the War of Independence. He's covered in blood, and his face is all black and blue."

"I am *not* your true love!" I tried to scoot away and almost fell off my sitting log. Mr. Clyman hooted.

"Not looking like that you aren't," Rosalie replied calmly. "Take off that filthy shirt and put this decent one on." She dropped a folded shirt of coarse white linen into my lap. She looked at my face again.

"Johnny," she asked, "what's to be done about his eye? It's swollen almost completely shut."

"I'm not wearing this shirt," I said firmly.

"His eye be good by and by," said Johnny. "No bleeding, and he see pretty fine. Just fancy colors. You like it tomor-row." He chuckled.

"Rosalie," said Mr. Clyman, "what does he owe you for the shirt? I'll see that he works it off."

"I'm not wearing this shirt."

"Well, I've done some thinking," Rosalie said. She sat down by Johnny and began pulling fresh biscuits from her apron pocket. She passed one to Mr. Clyman, one to Johnny. "See if you can make that disappear, magic Johnny," she said to him.

"I'm not wearing this shirt," I said. "And I'm not paying for it, either."

"I've been thinking," Rosalie continued. "This war shirt your friend Mr. Pickett wants. Men are so vain, I assume he will want it decorated with ermine and beads and scalps and whatnot."

"It's a fair guess," Mr. Clyman offered.

"And with quills, am I right?"

"I'd say so."

"Well, I have trade beads aplenty. And Mr. Pickett gave me a number of ermines himself. Now, if he wants scalps on there, he will have to acquire them himself, and I do not want to know about it."

Johnny saw where she was going, and he began to giggle.

"Quills," she said.

"Oh no," I said. "I am not . . ."

"Well, now," Mr. Clyman interrupted, "that sounds like a fair trade to me. We should be in good porcupine country by August. Will you be needing just one skin or two?"

"One will do nicely."

"Done," he said, slapping his knee.

"A pleasure doing business with you, Mr. Clyman," Rosalie said, standing up. "Johnny, you do nice work with a knife wound. Please try to keep him out of fights for a while."

"I keep an eye on him for you, miss."

She set three more biscuits on a flat stone by the fire, and then she strode away as briskly as she had come, while Mr. Clyman and Johnny doubled over with laughter. I didn't see what was so funny.

Seven

"Mr. Clyman, can I ask you a question?"

"What is it?"

The high warm sun shone down on ninety-four canvas-topped wagons that trailed out along the south bank of the Platte River. From where the sun stood, I imagined they looked like ants in a line, hauling dirty bread crumbs twice their size. I was leading the red mule, and Mr. Clyman rode his big gray horse at a walk beside me.

"When Mr. Haggard was going to take off my scalp, he called you 'Clements.'"

"Yes, he did," Mr. Clyman replied. "I haven't heard that name in some years."

"I have," I said.

"Have you, now? And where was that?"

"The Voice—whoever it was—that told me my pa was in trouble. He said something like, 'Clements is going out again,' and he also said, 'Clements will help you.'"

Mr. Clyman looked sideways at me. "Well," he said finally, "I don't mind helping you a bit. I guess you've been a help to me, too: that silly mule follows you like a pup."

"Who do you think it was?" I asked.

"Your Voice, you mean? One of the old-timers, I'd guess. There was a time when most all of us knew each other one way or another."

"But why 'Clements'?"

"Oh, people get a name sideways, now and then. Some of them called me Clements a long while back. I never cared for the name, myself, but Black Harris did, and he liked to pass it around as a joke. I guess old Haggard just never got it right. Haggard there, that isn't the name he was born to, either. Though I don't know what is."

An idea struck me then.

"Do you know my pa?"

"Etienne LeBlanc? Well, I know of him. Met him once at a rendezvous on the Popo Agie, or maybe Bear Lake. He likes the Seetskeedee country, I believe—or they call it Green River nowadays. That's south of Fort Bridger, where we'll pull up for a few days."

"I know. But what kind of trouble do you think he's in?"

He paused to think about it.

"Well, when the fur trade played out four years ago, a good number of the trappers didn't know what to do with themselves. Some went back East. Some went to California or Mexico or took up with the U.S. Army. Some settled in with the Indians—like Joe Meek or Toussaint

Charbonneau. Some just went bad—like Thompson Haggard." He looked over at me again.

"Now, don't get me wrong, boy, but Etienne LeBlanc has a dark side to him that you may not know about. I don't mean like Haggard, but still . . ."

"What *do* you mean?"

"Well, there are a few stories that he went a bit too native, that he ran a little too close with some of the war chiefs out there. I don't know if any of that is true, personally. But . . ." He stopped. "Well, hell, I might as well tell you this and get it off my chest. See, Daniel, I've known some fighting men in my day, but I never saw any like your pa. At one rendezvous I saw him deliberately provoke a four-man crew from the American Fur Company. They jumped him, just like he knew they would, and then he busted them up all by his lonesome. Two company men crawled away from that fight, and two others never moved again. Etienne LeBlanc was cut in about a hundred places, but he swung up on his horse and rode away singing a Blackfoot war chant. I never seen the like."

I was quiet.

"So it's hard to say what kind of trouble he'd be having that he couldn't handle himself. Unless he's just hurt and laid up somewhere."

"Can you help me find him?"

Mr. Clyman took his time. "Son, if you're bound to go after your pa, I can tell you where to look. I can point you.

But I've got to help these wagons get to Oregon, so I can't be out hunting with you. The other thing is, the odds are slim and none that you'll ever find him—especially if he doesn't know you're looking. You've got a few months of good weather left, and then you'll have to give it up for the winter. Depending on what kind of trouble he's in, that may be your last real chance, anyway."

I looked off toward the west, where the plains spread out in slow swells like a painting of the sea. The horizon was so far away, under so much sky. The wind pressed hard and warm and gritty against me, so that I felt sometimes it was wearing me away with its constant rubbing. To imagine myself alone out here made my mouth go completely dry. It gave me a blowing-away kind of feeling, as if my spirit itself might lift and rise. I looked away and tugged my hat down tight.

"It's a lonesome country, isn't it?" Mr. Clyman said.

"Yessir, it sure is."

"And then there's our old friend Scarface," he went on. "Near as I can guess, he was riding with a couple of Pawnee, looking to help himself to another few horses. That wagon train of sick folk said they lost about eight."

Mr. Clyman cleared his throat. "Haggard's wrong in the head, son. Now, he might plumb forget about you, or he might lay awake swearing to hunt you down. Or he might think you're charmed, and steer clear of you out of superstition. Point is, you don't know what he'll do. You've got away from him twice, but now it's different. Now he knows how to find you."

He coughed again and shifted in the saddle, looking back along the line of wagons behind us. "What I'm thinking is, you might be better off just heading back to Aunt Judith in Missouri. There should be an outfit in Fort Laramie moving eastward sometime soon."

I touched the swelling on the left side of my face. It was still tender where the skin was stretched over two big lumps. My hat was tight over the bandage around my forehead. For the second time, I had my doubts. But doubts are not anything I know how to work with. They just feel distracting to me. I took a big breath and let it out slowly.

"I believe I'll keep on westward," I said softly. "I need to find my pa."

Mr. Clyman nodded and was quiet for a few minutes.

"Well," he said finally, "we've got about four weeks till we hit the Green River country. Let's see what we can do to get you ready."

Eight

IT WAS our nooning, and I found a low bank along the Platte where I could get the red mule down to the water. I held his lead rope and let him wade out to where he liked it. He was a smart one, feeling his way along the hard ground until the water reached above his knees. Then he stopped and considered, like a deer would do. A drink, a pause, a sniff of the wind. A step or two, another drink, another step. I think he liked the water on his dusty legs, but he didn't want to get out too far, where he might have to swim. That would be too much like actual work.

I sat on the bank, dallying the rope and watching him take his time. Presently, his nose went up and his big mule ears twitched. I looked around for who might be coming. It was Rosalie, carrying a pair of wooden buckets.

"Good day, Mr. Red Mule," she said cheerily, ignoring me. "And how do you find the water today?"

"Ain't hard at all," I said in a mule voice. "You just walk down to the river and there it is. Hee haw, hee haw."

Rosalie smiled firmly as she set one of her buckets on the riverbank.

"Very funny," she said to him. "In fact, you may be the most amusing mule I've ever met." She moved upstream. The mule raised his nose to get a good whiff of her, then took a few steps in her direction. Rosalie drew her bucket through the stream, filled it, set it down, and picked up the empty one. The mule pushed his nose at her apron.

"What?" she asked him. "You don't really like biscuits, do you?"

She pulled a small yellow biscuit from her pocket and he took it from her hand with his lips. He made a great show of eating it, nodding and working his jaws. What a clown. Rosalie patted his cheek.

"Well, I've always got an extra one for you," she said.

She filled her second bucket and turned to go. The mule nodded along right after her, splashing out onto the shore and leaving his noonday bath behind. I got up with the lead rope in my hand.

"Here, give me the buckets," I offered. "He'd rather talk to you right now, anyway." We traded.

"Come along, Mr. Red Mule. We'll find some proper food for you," she said, patting his cheek again. I shook my head and trudged after them, lugging the water.

She picketed the mule in a windy patch of gramma grass where some of the other livestock were grazing while I spilled the buckets into the water barrel attached to the side of her family's wagon.

"The Parkers are not my real family, you know," she said. We walked toward a clutch of boulders where we could sit in some shelter from the wind. "I just work for them until I'm old enough to get out on my own. They give me thirty minutes' rest at nooning, and then whatever time is left in the evening after I get the supper cleared away. They let me take in sewing on my own, but I have to give them ten cents for every dollar I earn. I call that robbery myself."

"Where's your real family?" I asked.

"Gone," she said. She glanced away and then back at me. "I'll tell you, Daniel LeBlanc, because I trust something about you. But you must promise not to breathe a word of it to anyone. Mr. Parker is a reverend, and he would send me away without a second thought."

"Why?" I couldn't imagine what this girl's parents could have done that would be so terrible.

"You promise first," she said. Her brown eyes were wide and frank and intense. They looked directly into mine. "Promise."

"I promise."

"They would send me away because," she said, still searching my eyes, "I am half Indian."

"No, you're not," I said flatly, snorting. She was darker than me, but I'd never seen an Indian with freckles and curls. She slapped me right in the face.

"Don't you contradict me, Daniel LeBlanc. There is a long list of people I have to take that from, and I'm sorry but you are simply not on it."

I put my hand to my poor black-and-blue face; the imprint of her fingers stung over the lumps left by Haggard. My eyes watered and I sucked in my breath. I didn't think I had ever met anyone as fierce as this girl. I put my palm up, giving in.

"You're right," I said. "I'm sorry." She settled back a little, and then she began to pour out the words.

"My father was a trader named Angus McCulloch. He was a stout Scotsman with a dark red beard and curly hair, and I loved him dearly. I loved him in spite of all his shortcomings, which were many."

She glared at me, as if I were somehow at fault, too.

"He had a wife in Cincinnati. I am not sure, but I think he had another wife in St. Louis. He went up the Missouri River in the middle 1820s to work at Fort Clark, and he married my mother there. I don't think he wanted to, but it was part of some treaty agreement. I learned that from my mother, not from him. Anyway, my mother was Mandan, and our people have married white men for a hundred years. There are even blue-eyed Mandans.

"My mother's name was Song of the White Crane, and she gave Angus McCulloch four children, one of whom was me. I don't know how it happened, but I came out with her face and his curly hair. And since I landed with the Parkers, these curls are all that's kept me safe."

Rosalie was the youngest child of Angus and Song of the White Crane, born in 1830, same as me. Angus was especially attached to her. He taught her English, taught her to read and to cipher, and to speak her mind to white men. He often kept her in the trading post with him at Fort Clark.

From her mother, she learned the ways of her Mandan family. She learned about plants, which ones were good to eat and where to find them. How to care for the corn, and how to grind and cook it. She learned the ways of small animals and birds. On winter nights, while I was listening to Aunt Judith reading the scriptures in our cabin far to the south, Rosalie in the north was hearing stories in her grandmother's lodge. How the earth came to be; how a girl invented snowshoes; how one of her ancestors was a black bear in human form, and when he married a woman, the bear clan was started.

"That's impossible," I said.

"Hmmph," she replied. "You're just like Reverend Parker. You want to stamp out all the stories that don't come from the white world."

"I do not," I insisted. "It's just that a bear can't marry a woman."

"But you think an *angel* could marry a woman, right? Or a spirit?"

"Of course."

"Well, have you ever *seen* an angel?"

I had to admit I hadn't.

"Have you ever seen a bear?"

The problem was that I had seen plenty of bears, and after they've been shot and skinned, they really do look like humans. It's eerie.

"There you are, then," she declared. I was stumped.

In 1838, the Mandans and some of the Sioux tribes were going to war, and Rosalie's father was called back to St. Louis by his trading company. Two of her sisters had died of smallpox that spring, and the third one had been captured by the Sioux. When Angus left, he insisted on taking Rosalie with him. Song of the White Crane drowned herself in the Missouri River in the wake of the steamboat that took them away.

For five years, Rosalie lived in a Presbyterian boarding school in St. Louis. She saw her father twice a week. Sometimes he visited with a woman from St. Louis, whom Rosalie figured he had married. More often he came alone. At the school, Rosalie learned to cook, sew, and play the piano. She also read Shakespeare, the Bible, Plutarch, and even some books in Latin. Angus was very proud of her.

But then Angus stopped coming. The schoolmaster looked into it and found the notice of his death in a Cincinnati newspaper. Without the money that Angus had sent, the school could not keep her, so the master made arrangements to place her with the Reverend Parker, whose wife had a chronic ailment. They were heading out West.

"The Parkers want to set up a mission with the Indians in Oregon," she explained. "The Reverend thinks they have souls that must be saved, but he preaches hellfire and brimstone against marriage with them. It corrupts the purity of the white blood, he always says. So my schoolmaster, bless his heart, told the Reverend that I was half Italian." She shuddered. "I can't stand Mr. Parker."

"Why don't you leave, then?" I asked.

"Oh, don't be silly. Leave and do what? I'm a half-breed orphan girl in a white man's world."

Even I could see she had a point.

"So that's why you take in sewing?"

She brightened up about this.

"Yes, and that's going to be my way out. I have forty-five dollars saved, and I figure in two more years I will have enough to make a start on my own. I can find a boarding house in Oregon and keep up with expenses by sewing and tutoring. I was an excellent student—that's the other thing that saved me."

"And what about a husband?" I teased. "If you're fourteen, you better start looking."

She patted my hand and smiled her vicious smile.

"Well. Now that you've shown some better manners, maybe I'll put you back in the running. You can always hope."

I felt myself blushing again, from the collar of my new white shirt to the top of my sweaty white bandage.

Nine

Johnny and I stood watching two teenage boys fighting. They shoved and leaned on each other, swung wild haymaker punches, and tore each other's hair. Finally, one of them lowered his head like a bull and tried to lift the other over his shoulder. The second boy wrapped his arm around the neck of the first and began to choke him senseless. At that point, Johnny stepped in.

"Here, my friend, you don't want to kill your brother."

The boy was panting and grimacing, but still he bent over the other, choking him, forcing him to the ground. "Get away," he warned Johnny. "This ain't none of your business."

Johnny smiled in the most friendly manner. Then he put one hand on the back of the young man's head and very smoothly hooked two fingers under his jawbone. He almost lifted him off the ground. Releasing his brother suddenly, the boy grabbed Johnny's wrist with both hands and held on. He stood very still on the tips of his toes, gurgling quietly.

"I think it's maybe my English," Johnny said patiently. "My mother from Jamaica, and I don't say everything too clear. Now you understand better?" He raised his eyebrows in a question. "So. What happen to you, my friend, if you kill your brother by choking?"

The boy's eyes were full of pain, but he managed to whisper, "I see."

Johnny withdrew his hand, and the boy fell to his knees, gasping beside his brother. Johnny patted his shoulder, and we walked away.

"I remember you with Haggard," Johnny said to me. "You got the good instinct for small man fighting."

"For what?" I asked.

"You and me," he explained, "we small men. Mr. Clyman a very big man, yes? Mr. Haggard, he not so big but very strong."

I touched my bandage with one hand. Johnny went on.

"So Haggard holding his knife at your face. When he look around for me, you push his wrist away—good thinking. Wrist is small; arms is big. Also, Haggard's very strong hand in your hair. So I put my knife there"—he jabbed my shoulder—"Haggard let go. You drop down and get away. So—small man fighting."

"Like what you did with those boys just now."

"Yes, like that. Many small places hurt very bad. Eyes do, nose, under jaw, voice box, this place here." He touched me at the notch in my collarbone. "I press here, you don't talk for pretty long time." He poked gently, and I began to cough.

"Now, Mr. Clyman, he fight like a bear—crushing, pounding, breaking. Small man can't do that, right? So—we poke, we lever, change balance. Much different fighting," Johnny said. "I going to show you."

Every day at nooning and before supper, Johnny showed me. He knew more "small places" that hurt than I had ever imagined, and he patiently showed me, over and over.

"Many time, a big man grab your shirt. It's the big-man way. Very nice for you, really—it keep his hands busy."

He took my left hand and planted it on his own shirt.

"Good. Now he push or pull, right? Nothing else you can do with a shirt. I wait to see what you going to do."

I pushed.

"So you push," Johnny said, locking my wrist with his own left hand.

"And first I turn. . . ."

He pivoted sideways to me, and I was suddenly off balance, pushing a handful of shirt. He had my arm locked straight out in front of me.

"Next I hurt the elbow. . . ."

He tapped my elbow with his open right hand, sending a tongue of fire up my arm.

"Then I hurt the nose. . . ."

The back of his right fist stopped suddenly, half an inch from my nose. I bent backward to avoid it.

"Then maybe I hurt down here. . . ."

His fist disappeared from my nose and reappeared in front of my privates. I bent forward a little.

"Then I push you down."

He leaned on my arm again, and my forward motion took me down in a cloud of dust.

"Good," he said. "Now you."

I stood and began to brush off, but Johnny shoved me hard under the breastbone. I landed about four feet behind myself.

"Be ready," he warned. "We not dancing here."

He grabbed the front of my shirt and pulled me up. This time I was awake. I locked his wrist the way he had done to me, and I pulled back. Nothing happened.

"No," he said. "You got to go *with* him, not against him."

He yanked at me again, and I moved with him.

"Better. Now his heel, quick quick."

His foot lifted for a step back, and I hooked it. Down he went, slick as you please. I laughed.

"Be ready," Johnny said from the ground, and he hit me behind the knee with a heavy stick. I went down like a box of rocks.

"We not dancing here."

That is how it went, day after day. It became a way of thinking for me. Where is the balance? Where is the small place to hurt? I was spotted with bruises and lumps from Johnny's tutoring, but gradually I lost my fear of being grabbed. I lost the panic of pain. I learned to wait, to shift, to decide, to respond. I learned to be ready.

PART THREE

Fort Laramie

One

THE RED MULE had decided that we should find
Rosalie every morning and walk with her for the twenty
miles or so that we would cover in a day. Mr. Clyman didn't
much care where I walked, as long as I kept track of the
mule. This gave him a little more freedom to range afield
from the wagon train, to scout the trail ahead or do a little
hunting along the way. I would have tried to travel closer
to Mr. Clyman, but once we were ready to move in the
morning, the mule had his own ideas. He struck out for
Rosalie's wagon, towing me along whether I cared to go
that way or not. Both Rosalie and Mr. Clyman were highly
amused.

"Good morning, Mr. Red Mule," she'd sing out. "I hope
you had a pleasant night."

The mule would bump his nose against her arm until
she produced some small snack for him—a biscuit or a root
or fistful of sugar. Their little ritual finished, he was con-
tent to tag along with us as we walked beside the Parker
wagon.

"Your bruises are nearly gone," Rosalie said to me one morning. "Let me see the cut."

"It's fine," I said.

"I know, but let me see it."

I lifted my hat carefully and tipped my head down. Rosalie had a way of inspecting me that made me feel strange, like a child and a man at the same time. Her lips would purse slightly, and her eyes would narrow, as if she were judging the quality of a new shirt. She reached up to brush away a mosquito from my ear, and then she said, "Hold still."

Her left hand felt cool on my forehead as she plucked at something with her right. I watched her eyes, which were focused on the cut.

"There's a hair that's gotten stuck in the scab," she muttered, "and I just want to . . . "

"Ow!"

"Got it." She smiled then—not for me, but for fixing me—and she combed my hair away from the cut with her fingers. "Now you can put your hat on, and—wait!" She pinched at my hair again, then flicked something off her finger. "Ish. You've got fleas. All right, now the hat."

"Finally," I said. I was glad to put on my hat again and turn my blushing face away.

Mr. Clyman trotted up beside us on his gray horse.

"How does the war wound look today, miss?" he asked.

"Progressing nicely, Mr. Clyman," she replied. "I'm so impressed that it didn't fester."

"That would be Johnny's doing. His mother was a healer, and I'd say he learned a thing or two from her." Mr. Clyman bumped me with his foot. "I offered to make it a nice tattoo while we were at it, but your true love didn't want to do that. Something in the Good Book against it, I guess." He grinned at me.

"I am *not* her true love," I said. "This mule is. Anyway, a scar is plenty without a tattoo. Johnny and me will be twins."

Mr. Clyman grunted. "You could do worse."

Rosalie corrected me.

"Johnny and I," she said. "My father, rest his soul, used to say that a scar makes a man handsome and rugged-looking. But that is the most perverse sort of thinking I've ever heard. That would make our friend Mr. Haggard a very handsome fellow."

Mr. Clyman squinted.

"A man's scars are the writing on his body. They tell the story of his life."

"In that case," retorted Rosalie, "every life will be a story of pain, since pleasure doesn't leave a mark."

Mr. Clyman laughed out loud.

"She got me again. I swear, Daniel boy, I'd marry this girl myself if you weren't first in line."

I just groaned; I sure wished he would stop that.

"Which reminds me," he continued, "a few more days and we'll be in better porcupine country. Need to keep your eyes peeled when we get among the firs and spruce."

"Yessir," I said glumly. "Um, Mr. Clyman, I've seen plenty of quills, but I don't believe I've ever seen a porcupine."

"You don't get them back in Missouri so much," explained Mr. Clyman. "Well, maybe here and there. They like the cooler weather, and they like the evergreens."

"It isn't dangerous to catch them," Rosalie put in. "My mother used to catch them with my big sister."

Mr. Clyman chuckled. "Nah. I've seen some coyotes who wished they'd never tried, but if you don't bite them or fall on them, they're safe enough. They're built like a small beaver with a bad haircut, and they move about that slow, too."

"Why so slow?" I wondered.

"Same as a skunk, I guess," said Mr. Clyman. "Nobody wants to make them hurry." He smiled. Then he turned to Rosalie.

"You say your mother used to catch them?" he asked. "That wouldn't be in St. Louis."

Rosalie's eyes got big for one second, and then she reached up to brush a fly from the red mule's face.

"No," she said. "Before we moved there. So how do the mountain men catch them?"

"Best way is to sleep under a fir tree and let them crawl into bed with you."

I figured this was a tall tale coming up. "Right," I said. "And they'll make your tea in the morning, too."

"I have told a stretcher in my time," Mr. Clyman admitted, "but this isn't one of them. Many's the dark night I have woke to find a fat little nose pushing along my leg, or a fat furball trying to curl up on my ankles. There's a lot of mountain men who consider them quite good company."

I laughed.

"A match made in heaven," said Rosalie in her sweetest voice. "But I don't especially want to sleep with either one. I just want some quills to finish out Mr. Pickett's war shirt." She paused. "Thinking about your scar reminds me of something," she said to me. "Something about you and Mr. Haggard."

"What do you mean?"

"Oh, it struck me the other night. You look a bit like each other." She turned to Mr. Clyman. "I only saw him in the half-light, but didn't you think so?"

"That's crazy," I said. "I don't even want to think about that."

Mr. Clyman scratched the back of his neck and grinned out toward the horizon.

"I don't know," he said, teasingly. "Have to admit I had a similar thought."

I clenched my jaw and yanked on the mule's rope.

"I have no living relatives except Etienne LeBlanc and Aunt Judith Ruggles."

"They say everyone has a double somewhere," Rosalie offered.

"No," I growled.

"The Cheyenne say that every object casts a shadow," observed Mr. Clyman. "But don't you worry, son. He could be Johnny's shadow, for all we know. Porcupine's all the worry you need right now." He grinned again as he touched the gray horse into a trot and moved ahead of us.

"Morning, miss."

Rosalie chattered about her plans for Oregon, but I walked in silence with the red mule in tow. I was thinking of the bird silhouette my blanket made on the night I first saw Haggard.

Two

Fort Laramie was six hundred and thirty-five miles from Westport, Missouri, and I had walked every one of those miles on my own two feet. My boots had started out in good condition, but they were soon soaked through by the rain and the mud, and they had stayed wet for weeks. Gradually they dried as we walked along the Platte, and by the time we moved onto the High Plains, they were cracked and broken. The heels were sound, but the sole of one had come unstitched at the toe. The other one was starting to split across the top, where all the soaking and drying and bending had cracked it through.

Instead of wading in mud like we did all through Kansas, here we walked over the driest soil I'd ever seen. Here the earth was grit and crust, fine gray sand and limestone gravel. Every step raised a poof of dust. Plants were scarce, except for sage and bunchgrass, which seemed to love the hard climate. Aside from the Platte, water was scarce, too, though we could see ancient washouts everywhere. Mr. Clyman said maybe it was Noah's flood itself that gouged out the gullies and carved the high dry out-crops of stone. He said we were passing south of the Black Hills—a land the Oglalas thought was enchanted. The mountains there looked like skulls and towers and rounded castles. He said there was a graveyard of monsters, big as buffalo, with long, broad, scoop-shovel faces and horns on the sides of their jaw. He said there was a forest all turned to stone.

I thought the moon itself couldn't be more different from Caldwell, Missouri, than this land I was walking through.

And the wind blew without stopping. There were no trees to make it moan, but it kept up a low rushing sound, like a cyclone miles away. It would gather from hollows and rise over the high ground in a wash of air, sweeping away everything that wasn't tied down. The canvas on the wagons never stopped flapping. Our tents whipped and billowed like sails in the night. Our eyes grew tired from squinting. We jammed our hats down tight and got used to leaning into the wind as we walked mile upon mile. Johnny joked that if the wind ever stopped we would all fall down.

I read in a book once about the Moslems, who must cross the desert as an act of devotion sometime during their lives, to reach the city of Mecca. I thought of the Israelites, walking forty years in the wilderness, and of pil-grims in other books, who made their way to holy sites around the world. I glanced behind me, down the long trail climbing slowly over the High Plains. I sighed and turned forward once more and leaned into the wind. All I wanted was to find my pa and get him home again.

At our first glimpse of the mountains, the caravan came to a dead halt. Some of the men whooped and fired their guns and raced their horses back and forth. But most of us could only stare. We had been climbing steadily for days, till I thought the High Plains could go no higher, but the mountains—even from fifty miles away—seemed to gather the foothills like something handy for stepping from. I had expected high, tree-covered mounds, not these bursting, jagged continents of stone. They were too large for my mind to take them in. Yet in the morning light they were the colors of flowers: lilac, lavender, rose, with shadows of purple and blue. I have to say they frightened me, they disturbed me. I couldn't stop looking at them.

Mr. Clyman pulled up beside me and sat the gray horse for a moment, soaking in the sight. "I've been out here twenty years," he said quietly, "but it always makes my heart kind of wild just looking at them."

I plucked a rough yellow flower from the ground and held it close before my eyes, dragging the soft petals down my forehead, nose, and lips. I don't know why I did it. Maybe I was hiding. I was so small in my patches and my broken boots, and the mountains were so large, and beyond them, somewhere, my pa was in trouble. I felt dizzy and a little hopeless.

Three

Fort Laramie lay in a broad valley. A small, shallow fork of the North Platte River ran across our way through an open plain. Along the water to our left, a few dozen tepees stood, trailing woodsmoke from their open throats. Mr. Clyman said they belonged to a band of Oglalas who had come to trade at the fort. Shaggy horses were hobbled nearby. Some of the Oglalas smiled and gestured in our direction, as if they were joking with each other. We were ninety-four wagons, and every one was stuffed with more earthly goods than these Oglala folks had ever imagined owning or needing. I had to smile, too, at how hard these wagon families worked to make their lives easy.

The wagon road splashed through the shallow water and across the plain to the main gate of the fort. A tall square of upright timbers, whitewashed and plastered in mud, made the stockade, each wall running about a hundred and fifty feet. Above the main gate a square blockhouse with a pyramid roof surveyed the plain; a cannon looked out from a loophole. Other blockhouses kept watch at two corners of the stockade.

Our wagon train had not seen a town or dwelling made by whites for six hundred miles. We were excited by the stout look of the walls, by the pointed blockhouse roofs, by the cannon and the American flag. The fort seemed sheltered and safe. I tried to imagine what the Oglalas thought. Did the stockade walls keep them out or simply fence the white folks in?

The high-country air was almost too large for my lungs to breathe. I was used to Missouri, where the air had more weight to it, where the trees kept you from seeing too far, where the world seemed smaller and closer to the ground. I looked again at the stockade. Against its background here, Fort Laramie seemed like a short wooden castle, built by children.

The wagon captain didn't want our horses to tempt the Oglalas, so he ordered the wagons into three wide squares near the northeast corner of the fort. He would pasture the livestock safe in the center of each square. While the captain and the wagons got busy with that project, Mr. Clyman and Johnny decided to take a look around the fort. I went with them.

Inside the main gate, a wide passageway of rough wooden walls opened onto a square dusty parade ground. A knot of men bartering clogged the passage, and the three of us had to crowd past them on one side. On seeing Mr. Clyman, one of the traders peeled out of the group and strode up to us.

"James Clyman, you old reprobate, I thought the grizzly bears and the Pawnees had finally got rid of you. But here you come back again, older and uglier than what you was before!"

Mr. Clyman laughed out loud. "Wish I could say the same for you, Cletus," he said. "But I swear I've never seen you handsomer!"

I looked at him, a short beer barrel of a man, dressed in fringed buckskin pants and a wool shirt that had once been red but was now patched in many colors and blackened with grease and dirt. He wore a woven red sash over one shoulder, along with a battered powder horn. His bullet pouch looped over the other, and knife handles seemed to bristle from him like quills. He had tied charms in his stringy black hair—a swan feather, beads, a bear claw. A brass hoop hung from one ear. His thick black beard began just below his eyes, making his broad face seem oversized, bearlike. His nose had been broken or chewed. His eyes were set too far apart, and what few teeth he had were yellow and stood at odd angles. Mr. Clyman clasped him above the wrist and slapped his shoulder.

"Gentlemen," he said to Johnny and me, "meet Cletus McGee."

McGee scowled at us.

"You boys could do a heap better than tagging after this

old skinflint. Look how scrawny and worn he's let you get. You come on with me now, and let's get some meat on your bones."

The three of us walked with Mr. McGee across the square, past traders and Oglala men haggling in groups of three or four, past shaggy mountain horses, past a small campfire warming something in a pot. We stepped through a narrow doorway into a low room. The walls were hung with skins, giving it a snug, close, and warm feeling. An Indian woman sat on the floor, sewing in the light from a small window. Mr. Clyman thought she was from one of the Lakota tribes—possibly a Brule woman related to some of the Oglalas camped outside the fort. Her hands were small and quick, and she wore a loose dress made of buckskin. Unlike Mr. McGee, she had no sashes, patches, pouches, earrings, or good-luck charms decorating her. Her round face was dark and warm like cinnamon, and darker in the creases around her eyes. She had pulled her shiny black hair into two long braids. Mr. McGee said something to her, and she got up to stir the fire and take a large bundle from a hook on the wall.

"Got me a cast-iron stove, Clyman," Mr. McGee boasted. "Heavy one, too. Yessir, some pilgrim couldn't make it up South Pass last year, so he had to dump her. Right along the trail. Don't that beat all?"

"You're doing well," said Mr. Clyman. "I bet you wish there was more than buffalo chips to burn in it, though."

Mr. McGee hooted.

"Ain't that the truth! But, you know, I been cooking over chips so long I plumb got used to the flavor. One of these days, I guess I'll give up cooking and just eat the chips straight off the ground. Haw haw haw." When Mr. McGee laughed, his entire round body shook. The Lakota woman looked over at him skeptically.

She brought a large crock and put it on the dirt floor where we sat. Within the crock, a dozen rib bones thick with buffalo meat were piled, still sizzling from the fire, sending up the most delicious odors. She stood a moment behind Mr. McGee.

"Dig in, boys. It'll just draw the flies in a minute," said Mr. McGee. "Hump rib's the best, ain't it, Clyman? But I et that yesterday. Haw haw haw. Didn't know you was coming."

A shaft of light from the window crossed Johnny's hand as he reached for a rib, and the woman shrieked. We all froze as she stared, wide-eyed, speaking rapidly in a high voice. Mr. McGee began to laugh so hard his face went red and he started choking. Mr. Clyman turned to Johnny.

"She's impressed with *you*, Johnny," he said.

"I see," Johnny replied, smiling. "And who can blame her, eh? I quite the impressive fellow."

He held up his hand in the sunlight, for the woman to inspect. First the palm, callused, pink, and lined in warm browns. Then the back of his hand, dark as chicory and buffalo hide. The woman wanted to touch him, and Johnny nodded. She began to mutter as she inspected his hand. Johnny turned it over, and there in his palm was a tiny brass bell, winking golden in the sunlight. The woman shrieked again, and Johnny made it disappear. Mr. McGee roared with laughter; he fell on his back and pounded the floor. The woman smiled. She reached for Johnny's hand again, turned it over. Nothing. Turned it back, and there was the brass bell again. Her face lit up. She lifted the bell and jingled it. Johnny took his hand away.

"Aw, don't give it to her," teased Mr. McGee. "Now she'll be after me for a trinket every time she sees a colored man! Haw haw haw!"

"I think she don't see that many." Johnny smiled. "You probably very safe about that." The woman spoke to Johnny in a long stream of rapid words, and gestured toward the bowl of buffalo ribs. Johnny nodded and quickly reached for one. "Yes, yes," he said. "I eating."

Four

"**W**HAT ARE YOU reading?"

"Nothing much."

Rosalie sat down beside me and turned my book to see the cover. *"The Tragedies of William Shakespeare."*

"It's Mr. Clyman's," I said. "He's letting me borrow it."

Mr. Clyman had two or three books with him. He liked poetry, he liked Shakespeare, and he had a ledger where he kept accounts for the crew—what they earned, what they borrowed. He had a journal, too, where he wrote his daily thoughts about the company, the land we were passing through, the ladies. Even some poems.

"Why are you so shy about reading, Daniel LeBlanc?" she asked.

"I don't know. Because of the men in the crew, I guess. They say it's just for dandies."

"These are the men who can't write their names or count their own pay, am I right?"

"I guess so."

"Well," Rosalie said simply, "that explains why Mr. Clyman is in charge of keeping their accounts."

She pulled out the war shirt she was making for Pickett and began stitching beads to a rectangle of red trade cloth that made the neck flap.

"How did you know how to make a shirt like that?" I asked her.

She waved a hand. "Oh, it's easier than it looks. My grandmother made me help her lots of times. Also, I saw a few in St. Louis—on some of my father's greasier friends." She held up the shirt to frown at it. "Besides, it's in the blood. Now, I would have made this neck flap a triangle. But Mr. Pickett wants it Crow-style, so he says that means a rectangle. Hmm."

I didn't like to admit it, but I did enjoy being with Rosalie. She had something—an air about her, maybe—that I wished I could have, too. It was as if she never doubted herself; she took in her life at one swift glance, and she knew exactly what to do.

"Don't stare at me," she scolded. "Read me some Shakespeare instead."

I blushed. "No, I won't read Shakespeare to you. You're the excellent student, but I can't even say half these words."

"Try," she commanded.

"But look at this: 'Alas! poor ghost.' No, wait, I can get that part."

I flipped a page.

"Right here. See, the ghost is talking, and he says it would 'make thy two eyes like stars start from their spheres . . . and each particular hair to stand on end like quills upon the fretful porpentine.' I can't follow this kind of talk."

Rosalie didn't look up from her beading. "He just means it would scare you. Make your eyes bug out and your hair stand up."

"Oh," I murmured, beginning to understand. "That's good. All right, what about this part: 'But know, thou noble youth, the serpent that did sting thy father's life now wears his crown.' And then Hamlet says, 'O my prophetic soul! My uncle!' What does all that mean? I thought he was explaining a secret, but a snake wearing a crown? That would be pretty hard to miss. Sounds like one of my pa's tall tales."

"It's his uncle."

"What?"

Rosalie shifted the beadwork on her lap and tipped it toward the firelight.

"Hamlet's uncle is the snake. The ghost is saying that the uncle killed the father and took the crown. We played this last spring for the parents."

"You were in a play?"

"Mm hmm."

I looked at the page again. Sure enough, it all began to take shape in my mind.

"'Murder most foul . . . ,'" I read. "'O villain, villain, smiling, damn-èd villain!'" Suddenly I was shaking. *Your daddy's in trouble, boy.*

"Kings are always killing each other," Rosalie declared.

Your daddy. You know how to find him? I closed the book.

"I don't think Aunt Judith wants me reading cuss words."

Rosalie laughed.

"You look like you've seen a ghost. Well, it all reminds me that you still owe me a clutch of porpentine quills."

"What?"

"Quills, handsome." She held the shirt up.

I was still shaken by the ghost of Hamlet's father when Johnny came back. He and Mr. Clyman had been in the fort to trade. But now the evening was growing dark, and the trading had turned to drinking and shouting. Johnny never stayed too long when the white men started drinking.

"Why so quiet?" he teased. "You and Miss Rosalie supposed to be arguing all the time."

Rosalie laughed, but I didn't see what was funny.

"Any good trades at the fort?" I asked Johnny.

"Sure, sure," Johnny answered, squatting by the fire. "Good trades for the fort, not for the wagons. Pint of sugar be one and a half cent; pint of flour, one cent. Barrel of flour take forty dollar. Yow. Some wagon ladies not amused one bit."

Johnny chuckled. Then his face froze, and he cocked his head, listening.

"What is it?" whispered Rosalie. I sat up and listened, too.

Johnny was looking toward me, but not looking at me. Without turning, he raised one hand slowly to the side and beckoned with it. From that direction, a small figure emerged, and then Rosalie and I heard it—the tinkle of a tiny brass bell.

Five

"LET ME TRY," said Rosalie. "I used to know some of the hand signs."

She leaned toward the Lakota woman and made a few slow, careful gestures with one hand. The woman's eyes went from Rosalie to Johnny and back to Rosalie. She answered with several gestures of her own.

"Her name is South Wind Woman," Rosalie said, "and she says we're in danger."

Rosalie made a quick motion, and the woman repeated slowly. One sign that looked like something taken and something given, then three distinct gestures.

"Someone traded something," Rosalie murmured. "Then she says there's a mountain man, then something I don't know, then something about 'boy.'"

She mimicked the sign in the middle, and South Wind Woman repeated. Rosalie still didn't get it. The woman hissed. She stood and crossed over to Johnny. She made the sign again and slapped his chest. She went back and sat down.

Rosalie raised her eyebrows and went slowly through the signs again, whispering.

"Someone traded. Mountain man. Colored man. Boy." The woman said one word and dropped her hands.

"Right," said Rosalie, barely breathing.

Rosalie made the sign for question.

"Who traded?" she asked.

With one finger, South Wind Woman drew a line down the left side of her face.

"Daniel, my friend," said Johnny softly, not taking his eyes from the woman. "Mr. Clyman close by. You go find him very quick."

"I'm here." Mr. Clyman's voice came in from one side. I was always astonished at how softly he moved for a man his size. He squatted beside South Wind Woman and spoke a few words in the Lakota language. She talked rapidly, sometimes repeating the gestures she had used with Rosalie.

"Well, that Cletus McGee," Mr. Clyman said. "According to her, he's supposed to knock me and Johnny in the head, and sell off Daniel to the Utes. I knew about Haggard, but I sure didn't know Cletus was mixed up in slaving. She says he's done it before with wagon-train children. Hmph. He must think I'm pretty easy to outfox, is all I can say."

Mr. Clyman stood and said a few terse words to the woman. She stood, too, and stepped over the sitting log. Then she turned back to say something more, looking at Johnny as she spoke. He listened hard.

"South Wind a good name for this woman," Johnny said. "Almost I read her, but everything moving, everything in colors, in bigness or brightness—no names, just how things look." He sighed, still watching her. "Very exciting language, but very hard for me."

Something went by me very fast. I heard a thick little buzz like a hummingbird, and then South Wind Woman fell down. Mr. Clyman and Johnny leapt out of the light, and Rosalie threw herself down behind the sitting log. I knew I should do something, but everything moved so slowly for me.

"Daniel!" It was Rosalie's voice. "Get down!"

I took one step and tripped over the tea kettle. The tea spilled into the fire and sent up an explosion of ash and steam and smoke. I heard the buzzing sound again, and something hit the ground near my rump. I scrambled away on all fours. Something else hit the sitting log near Rosalie, and then I heard yelling and running feet. Those sounds faded quickly, and everything was quiet except for South Wind Woman breathing rapidly and hissing through clenched teeth.

Six

She must have been turning when the arrow struck her, because it missed her throat and drove through the slope of flesh between her neck and her shoulder. Rosalie helped her sit up against the log, and used a square of blue cloth to wipe at the blood that was running down her back and spilling over her collarbone in front. The head of the arrow had gone through and now it dangled and waved behind her, while the shaft was still caught in her flesh by its own fletching. My stomach did flips, and I must have gone green in the face. Rosalie pushed me away.

"Fix the fire, Daniel," she ordered. "Fill the kettle with clean water and get it boiling." I was glad to do something other than stare at the blood. As I worked, Rosalie spoke in a soft voice, sounding calm and efficient. South Wind Woman moaned quietly from time to time and hissed in pain when she breathed. She kept her eyes on Rosalie's face.

"Oh, good job. She still with us."

South Wind Woman turned her head at Johnny's voice, but jerked back immediately with a yelp. Johnny knelt down in front of her and smiled. He jingled the little bell on its thong around her neck.

"You try to help us and get shot for the trouble. I don't like that."

"What do we do about this arrow, Johnny?" Rosalie asked. "It's got to come out."

"Sticking in the bone or just the muscle?" he asked, still smiling at South Wind Woman. She breathed easier now, relieved to see him.

"Missed the bone," muttered Rosalie, inspecting it. She dabbed at the blood again.

"Can you break?"

"I tried, but the wood's too tough for me. And very slick from the blood. Also, it hurts her when I touch it."

Johnny spoke to the woman.

"We got to pull that arrow through," he explained. He made a pulling motion with his hands and nodded to her shoulder. She sighed and looked away.

"Daniel," said Johnny, "you come hold her steady in front. I going pull it out back there."

I sat on the ground facing South Wind Woman and locked wrists with her, my feet braced on the log beside her hips. Johnny stepped behind her. Immediately she began to argue. She let go of my wrists and waved her hands, speaking in a rapid tumble of words. She turned as much as she could to find Johnny.

"What?" he asked. "What we doing?"

She continued to argue and gesture. Finally, Johnny understood.

"Yes, you think that be better? Fine." He waved me up. "Trade places: I hold the South Wind, you pull out the arrow."

He sat down and took South Wind Woman's wrists as I had done.

"Me?" I said. "Johnny, I can't do that. I'll just make a mess of it; I'll hurt her."

"I be right here, and she already hurt," he said. "You do what I say and you be careful. Now go."

I looked at the slippery shaft of the arrow, wondering where to hold it. My pa had told me stories about this, but I never thought I would have to live through it myself. Rosalie handed me the blue cloth.

"Here," she said. "Wrap this around the arrowhead. You can pull with that."

I wrapped the head carefully, but South Wind Woman hissed when the arrow moved.

"It fine, it fine, squeeze my wrist," Johnny murmured to her.

"Johnny, I can't do this," I said, dropping the rag. "My stomach is turning over."

Johnny scowled. He stood up and reached across the log gently to take my wrist. A quick motion, and pain flashed upward to my shoulder. I gasped; my eyes watered.

"Daniel!" Johnny barked into my ear, still holding my wrist. "You stomach gonna be the only part that *don't* hurt.

Now you take hold and you pull that arrow *out*. We *not* dancing here."

"Yessir," I whispered.

Johnny sat down again, and I turned back to the arrow. Gingerly I wrapped the blue cloth around the head again.

"Ready, Daniel? Now you stand on one foot and put other foot beside this lady backbone. Got it?"

"Got it," I said through my teeth.

"Good boy, Daniel," he said calmly, looking at South Wind Woman. "Good job. Now feel the balance. You know how. Now, you want to pull with arms only, not pushing with foot. Feel the balance. Be a tree, my friend . . . grow roots . . . and bring in the arrow from the South Wind. Heh heh."

"Yessir," I said. I was sweating, thinking hard about roots. Johnny's eyes never left South Wind Woman's face while he spoke to me.

"Now pull quick and smooth, arms only, when I say."

"Yessir."

Gradually, I felt my legs go solid while my arms stayed loose and light. My mind was empty except for this arrow tight in my hands and Johnny's voice.

"Ready. And. Go."

My hands snapped back to my hip, and the arrow was out. Rosalie moved in with a clean cloth to press against the blood, as South Wind Woman fainted and fell forward onto Johnny. I stood staring at the bloody stick in my hands while Johnny laughed and laughed.

Seven

CLETUS MCGEE had sold us out—that much I understood. But I didn't follow the hows and wherefores. Mr. Clyman tried to explain it to me while Johnny worked on South Wind Woman's shoulder and Rosalie watched.

"If you're asking why Cletus sold us out," Mr. Clyman said, "only Cletus and good old Scarface will know that. But we know that Haggard wants you, boy, because you caught him thieving horses and you almost shot him in the rump. He wants me because I put the word out, and now he can't slip quietly back to Missouri. He wants Johnny because Johnny's knife kept him from getting your scalp. By now, I figure he wants just about everybody we've ever spoken to. It's always bound up with payback for Haggard. He's not much of a thinking man, and I don't guess he can help it, but when somebody frustrates him, they generally lose their hair. So now the fever is on him, and he'll likely follow us clear to Oregon. That is, unless somebody else makes him even madder."

"Maybe Cletus McGee don't want to be the one," Johnny put in. "Hard to say no to Haggard."

"Yep. Or else Cletus owes him something. He's a betting man, Cletus is. Anyway," Mr. Clyman declared, "we know Haggard is somewhere up the trail, and now Cletus has disappeared from the fort. So that means they'll both be laying for us between here and Oregon."

"But I'm not going to Oregon," I said. "I'm going down the Green River to find my pa."

Rosalie shot me a look, and Mr. Clyman cleared his throat.

"Son, I'll tell you what," he said. "Heading down there would be about the most simpleminded thing you could do right now. That's Haggard's own territory. I think he and his pals run horses and guns from there on down to Santa Fe. And they run a few slaves, too. Sell them to the Utes or the Spanish. You'd best be coming along with us."

I thought about that. Haggard gave me nightmares. But some things were more important than Haggard. *It's up to you from here,* the Voice had said.

"I'm sure your pa is a good man," Mr. Clyman went on. "So is Cletus McGee, at bottom. But good men and bad men get all mixed up on the frontier, and they tend to rub off on each other. One thing, though—there aren't any heroes. Trying to be a hero is a sure way to get lost or get killed out here, boy."

"I'm not trying to be a hero," I snapped. "I just mean to find my pa."

I could feel the anger building up in me again. "I'm sorry, Mr. Clyman," I said. "You've been mighty kindly toward me. I'm sure I owe you my life. But I have walked on my own two feet from Caldwell, Missouri, all the way to hell and past, aiming to find my pa. Now, I believe he's down the Green River, and I do not figure to walk right by him for Oregon or anyplace else!"

I sat poking the fire, and nobody said another word for a long time.

Eight

"WHAT DID YOU USE to make this, Johnny-the-Healer?" Rosalie asked. She was dabbing a poultice on South Wind Woman's shoulder, where the arrow had gone in and come out. "And why didn't you just make the arrow disappear? Some magician you are."

Johnny laughed. "I been busy holding hands." He loved it when Rosalie teased him. "Poultice is lizard-tail plant, mostly—you know that one? Picked it in Kansas. A little alumroot, too; I think that squeeze off the blood."

He leaned over to inspect Rosalie's work.

"Good. Now you bind up, please." He chuckled. "You bind up the South Wind." Johnny always found the line between serious and joking. I don't know how he did it.

Rosalie bound the wound, and then she went off to pack up the Parker family wagon. Mr. Clyman had left early in the morning on the gray horse. Fort Laramie had supplied the caravan all it had to offer, and we were getting ready to head westward again. I can't say I was sorry to leave.

The next settlement we would see was to be Fort Bridger, and it would take us three or four weeks to reach it. From there, I would take a branch of the Green River and travel south to where I would find my pa. Wherever that was. I tried not to think about that part. I tried to keep only the Voice in my mind. The rest of it—the rivers, the wilderness, the way—would take care of itself. My job was to walk.

The high-country air was fine and cool, and I found myself beginning to like the largeness of it as we pulled away from Fort Laramie. We rolled over dry hills, some of them chalk white in the sun. Shrubby cedars and pines dotted their sides, living on what moisture I didn't know. Mr. Clyman found a spring and a small river for the wagons to camp beside the first night. I could feel the mood of progress and determination and high spirits moving through the travelers, like I hadn't felt it since before the rains along the Kansas River.

A brief squall passed over us the first night, but next morning the sun rose in what Mr. Clyman called "beautifull majestie over her parched cliffs." I read this in his journal before I packed it away on the red mule that morning. I wished I had his way with words.

South Wind Woman left Fort Laramie with us. Usually she walked to the side and a little behind Johnny on his horse. When he was gone scouting with Mr. Clyman, she walked with Rosalie near the Parkers' wagon. Some of the white people argued that an Indian shouldn't be allowed to travel with us, but Reverend Parker took up her cause. He scolded them in his finest church-house style, saying that the Lord had brought this savage child of the wilderness to us as an emblem of our duty to seek and to save that which was lost. Rosalie said later that she had lied to Mr. Parker, telling him that she was giving South Wind Woman the gospel in sign language as they walked.

Late on our third day out of Fort Laramie, we climbed to the head of an uncommonly green valley and broke out of the trees onto a wide ridge that sloped away to the north. On the west, a tremendous range of mountains rose like the purple backbone of the earth. And to the east, our ridge fell away sheer into a limestone canyon, a thousand feet to the bottom and half a mile across. I could see a river down there, passing slowly through a wild range of stone knobs and humps that looked for all the world like a jumble of giant mushrooms. It was a magic land.

We crossed four streams of clear, sweet water and pulled up to camp at the western edge of a broad valley.

In the evening, I took my knife and rifle and walked away from camp by myself. I went quietly, stopping often to listen. I didn't want another surprise like the one along the Platte.

Maybe a half-mile to the west, I dropped down into a hollow and suddenly came upon a ring of skulls on the ground. Buffalo skulls. I counted twenty-four of them, each one larger than the circle of my arms, and there was one skull that looked to be a wolf's. They were laid out in a perfect horseshoe shape, their eye sockets staring empty toward the center. Only the wolf skull at the top of the arc was facing outward.

A full moon was rising in the east, turning the skulls the palest green, and suddenly I knew I had stumbled into a holy place. I stood for a moment, scarcely breathing. Then, before I knew what I was doing, I stepped through the opening and into the middle. I set the wolf skull right. The moon shone down, and I raised my face to it. I stepped back, opened my arms, and turned one slow full turn in the center of the ring. Then I settled on my knees and closed my eyes to listen.

I don't know what I heard. Words, but not in any human language. Sounds of heavy movement, shuffling hooves, and the grunting of large animals. I began to feel cold, and then like I was floating. I tried to breathe like Johnny taught me. The top of my head tingled, and the shapes of buffalo shambled through my mind. I felt as if the wind was passing through me, and for a moment I thought I should run away.

After the buffalo, there came a parade of burning wagons. Then the devil, wearing his black hat and Haggard's long scar. My pa was there, painted in soot and blood, and calling *"bouge pas,"* don't move. I forced myself to breathe, taking huge, slow gulps of air. Then the ground heaved and shook as the buffalo staggered past me again. This time they were chased by soldiers in blue coats, shouting and shooting. And the buffaloes' heavy bodies crashed into the dust until the ground was covered in pale green skulls like cobblestones from giant cities.

Mountains came into view, and a whitewashed stockade. I felt the wind blowing from the ridges, and riding the wind I saw arrows, flaming arrows like bolts of lightning. Now there were soldiers dying on the ground, Indians falling from the backs of shaggy horses, and tepees and buildings going up in flames. I saw Haggard laughing like a madman while he waved a raw scalp in the air.

Then a face slowly began to take shape in front of me. It was massive, silver-white and shiny under the moon, and I saw the hungry eyes open slowly and take me in. A wolf. He tossed his head and he said something fierce in the language I didn't know. I kept still while he stared at me long and hard. Then he spoke one word in a voice I have known all my life.

"Daniel."

It was the voice of my father. My eyes flew open, and I was alone.

Nine

Rosalie sat with South Wind Woman by the fire, leaning over a piece of handwork. She had learned to speak a few words of the older woman's language, but mostly she used hand signals and spoke English, while South Wind Woman replied in Oglala words and some of the English that she must have learned from Cletus McGee.

They were working with porcupine quills. South Wind Woman had a number of them laid out near a small bladder pouch on the ground. They had been flattened and dyed red, and she was piecing them one by one into a round design that looked like it might become part of a necklace. South Wind Woman glanced up at me when she realized I was watching. She said something sharp to Rosalie and made a sign with her hand.

"Daniel, don't stare," Rosalie said. "This is woman stuff; you shouldn't even be here."

I never understand women when they get like this. How could there be some ways that belonged to them and not to men? I tried to imagine two men shushing Rosalie and sending her away: "Go on, girl, we're molding bullets." I had to laugh at the idea. Fur would fly.

I picked up a twig and smoothed a place in the dirt to draw. Twenty-four small triangles in a horseshoe, with their points to the center. Twenty-four small pairs of horns on each triangle. One smaller triangle at the top of the arc. I sat back to look at it. A ring of buffalo skulls.

"So you found it, did you?" It was Mr. Clyman. "I wondered if you would."

"What is it?" I asked him. Johnny sat down beside me.

"Don't really know," said Mr. Clyman. "Sort of magic circle that some of the tribes use. I've only seen a few of them myself. This one happens to be close along our way."

"Would South Wind Woman know?"

"We could ask her, but I doubt she'd tell us."

"Would she tell Johnny?"

"There's a thought. Why don't you try her, Johnny?"

Rosalie and South Wind Woman were putting away their red quills, now that so many men were invading. Johnny motioned to her and pointed at my drawing on the ground. South Wind Woman came to look. At first she was surprised, then she turned away quickly and sat down again by Rosalie. She said something short to Mr. Clyman. He translated for us.

"She says it's nothing. A game for children."

"I think not," said Johnny. "Very secret thoughts in her now."

He watched her closely as Mr. Clyman spoke to her again. South Wind Woman looked at Johnny as Mr. Clyman spoke, her eyes wide and cautious. Johnny laughed.

"What did you say about him?" asked Rosalie, suspiciously.

"He say I be great magic," Johnny answered.

Mr. Clyman grinned. "Something like that. The Lakota have stories about a magic fellow who changes shape sometimes. Iktomi. He's a good fellow, usually, but he'll trick you. I said you were the Iktomi of the colored people."

Johnny drew his eyebrows together and scowled at South Wind Woman. The perfect scars on his cheeks caught the light in a way that made them glow, and his eyes stood out brightly. His face became a mask of dark magic.

"Now you tell Gianni Shape Changer what this circle mean," he growled. South Wind Woman shifted in her seat, and she wouldn't look at Johnny. She caught Rosalie's wrist in her hand. Rosalie snorted.

"Don't tell them a thing," she said. She picked up a heavy stick and waved it at all three of us.

"You stay away! Bullies!"

South Wind Woman was shocked. She tried to slap the stick away from Rosalie, shushing her and motioning at Johnny nervously. But Rosalie fended her off.

"No! They're just men! They're bullies! Don't you tell them anything!"

Mr. Clyman and Johnny were quiet. Johnny sat back on his heels and put up his hands. He smiled at South Wind Woman.

"No, you don't tell me," he said. "I don't trick it from you."

"You do and you'll be sorry," Rosalie growled. She still had the stick.

"Mr. Clyman," I said, "could you tell her I had a dream in the skull circle?"

He became very still.

"A dream," he said. It wasn't a question.

"I think it was a dream."

Johnny was listening, too.

"Yes, something happen to you," he said.

Mr. Clyman spoke to South Wind Woman, more gently this time, and she turned to look at me. She asked Mr. Clyman a question.

"What was your dream?" he translated.

"Buffalo." I thought that was close enough.

"Tatanka," said Mr. Clyman.

South Wind Woman relaxed. She spoke rapidly to Mr. Clyman and shrugged.

"She says that sometimes hunters call the buffalo from circles like that. It's what I've heard before."

"And soldiers," I said. "And a wolf."

Mr. Clyman translated. South Wind Woman made her face completely blank, and she spoke a few very serious words slowly and directly to me. I felt I was being scolded by Aunt Judith.

"She thinks white boys shouldn't play in medicine circles. That's all she wants to say."

I didn't say any more, either.

PART FOUR

Green River

One

WE TRAVELED UPWARD for a week or more, until we came to South Pass. High in the mountains, above the timberline, the country was almost bare of plants. The sun was fierce during the day, but at night the mountain air left frost on the ground. Patches of snow were everywhere, and we melted it for water. We saw buffalo moving in groups of twelve or more, and antelope, coyotes, grouse, and elk. Along the small streams we crossed, we saw signs of grizzly bears. What grasses there were had been grazed down by the buffalo, and the antelope seemed to like the wild sage plants. The ground was dry and gravelly, and our own dust followed us in clouds.

South Pass was a high mountain pass that Mr. Clyman and other mountain men had found twenty years before. It was well known to the Indians, and now the white emigrants used it on their way to California and Oregon. To reach it, we had to travel along the creeks, which cut through high granite cliffs on either side. At one point, the canyon closed in so tight to the stream that we thought some of the wagons might not be able to squeeze through.

There were signs of other caravans that had passed this way ahead of us, and soon we caught up with one that was camped along the Sweetwater River. It was the train of invalids we had met before Fort Laramie. They had been pulled up for a week to repair broken wagon wheels and axles, and because one of the men was too sick to move. He died of typhus the night we arrived, and they buried him the next morning. Mr. Clyman said someday there would be a grave every twenty yards along the Oregon Road. I wondered if there would be broken axles and rusted stoves and the trash of wagon camps every twenty yards, too. *Cochons*, I could almost hear my pa say. *Pigs.*

Next afternoon, one of the men came running into camp, shouting that he'd seen a grizzly bear in the aspens across the river. Mr. Clyman asked if the bear had hurt anyone, but he hadn't. Never mind that, they all said, he's a bear. So seventeen men grabbed their guns and horses and charged off to find him. Across the stream and into the aspens they went, over deadfalls and rock piles, crashing into each other, swearing, and shooting. The gunfire sounded like a small war.

I saw the bear when they flushed him out of the brush, and the sight took my breath away. His coat was a deep rust color with flashes of silver hair along his hump. He was big as a horse, but his body was loose-limbed, streaming blood down his left foreleg, where someone had hit him with a rifle ball. But the wound didn't seem to slow him down. Eight men stumbled after him on horseback, firing their guns, but even with only three legs, he was outrunning them. Uphill.

The men came back shortly, winded and unhappy. The grizzly had run into some thick willows farther upstream, and the men couldn't get their horses to follow him. One horse had broken its knee running through the stream, and it had to be shot. Another horse had been notched in the ear by a rifle ball. Another was grazed across the rump. The men had various sprains and scuffs from the rocks and the brush. One of them was bleeding from a scratch on his eye. And two of them were ready to fight, because one had fired at the other accidentally in all the confusion.

"All in all," Mr. Clyman said quietly, "that there was a typical greenhorn bear hunt."

After supper, I walked out along the riverbank to see where the commotion had been. A narrow game trail wandered through the brush, joined from time to time by other trails coming in from the sides. Compared with the dry mountain air we'd been walking through, the breeze along the river was green with moisture. I sucked in the smell of leaves and moss and mud and animal dung like perfume. I followed the sign of buffalo, antelope, and elk where they came to the water. In the soft earth of the riverbank, the tracks looked like letters in a book, all tightly stamped together to tell a story.

I knelt down by one of the grizzly's tracks. It was larger than my hand where his pads had pushed the mud out wide. I pressed my palm into the hollow of his track and stretched my fingers out to touch his claw marks one by one. My scalp tingled.

"Sure was a big one, wasn't he?"

I spun around and something knocked me flat on my stomach. Before I could roll over, a heavy knee pinned my shoulder to the ground and a hard hand yanked my head back by the hair.

"It's me again, white boy," breathed Haggard in my ear. "Don't say you're not glad to see me."

Two

I STUMBLED as Haggard dragged me up the game trail to a sandy patch in a small stand of aspen. He bound my wrists together and then tied them to a rope he had looped over a limb high above my head. In minutes I could feel the blood leaving my arms, and my hands were getting cold. He shoved a dirty wad of buckskin into my mouth and tied it behind my head.

"Don't go away," he whispered, grinning with all three of his teeth. Then he disappeared.

It was growing dark. The leaves trembled and rubbed together lightly in the breeze, and the river made constant washing sounds over the rocks—just loud enough to cover any moan or bark that I might make around the gag in my mouth. My arms were going numb from lack of blood, and I dearly wanted to do something about that. I tried to make my mind very still. I tried to think without panic, like Johnny had taught me.

The tether to the tree limb didn't yank my arms up tight; it was just short enough so that I couldn't lower them. If I stood on my toes, I could gain an extra inch or two of slack and flip the tether back and forth. It wouldn't loosen. I tried to shinny up the rope, but that just waved the limb up and down. I tried pulling harder to see if I could break the limb, but it was a little too sturdy for that. I stopped to pant and listen. Nothing.

My tether was just long enough to reach the trunk of the tree. I tried to pull against it while I shinnied up the trunk, but with the rope behind me, it was impossible. I fell off twice before I thought to try the far side of the tree. From there, the tether pulled me against the trunk instead of away from it, and I was even able to brace with my hands a little. By the time I climbed to my tether limb, the blood was back in my arms, and the rope hung down in a loop halfway to the ground. I stopped again to listen before I inched out onto the branch. Still nothing.

I sat astride the limb with my back to the tree and reached out as far as I could toward where the rope was tied. As long as most of my weight had been on the rope it held tight, but from here I had plenty of slack to loosen Haggard's loop and slip it toward me along the branch. I untied his knot and let the rope fall. I couldn't bend my wrists to get at the knots around them, but at least I could walk back to the wagons now. I scrambled down the tree. I was coiling up the tether so it wouldn't drag in the brush when I heard them coming.

I knew Haggard by his laugh, and I thought there was another man. There was the sound of someone struggling, and then the laughter of the two men again. I slid into the brush and worked my way toward the downhill side of the clearing to watch. I could be on the trail at a dead run in two steps.

Haggard came into view first, then the other two. One was Cletus McGee, but the other one was covered with a blanket, with only hands exposed—bound as mine were. Haggard stopped for a second when he saw that the rope and I were gone, but then he walked straight to the tree. He sized it up very quickly, and followed my tracks toward the brush with his eyes.

"That's good work, white boy," he called. How he guessed I was close enough to hear, I don't know. His eyes searched for me but passed over my hiding place. "But before you run off, I want you to think about something." Haggard drew his knife and stepped over to the prisoner. He yanked off the blanket.

It was Rosalie.

"Before you go, little mountain man," Haggard sneered, "think about the white girl you're leaving behind. With me." He laughed. He had the knife in one hand and Rosalie's hair wrapped in the other. His eyes raked the brush for me. Rosalie kicked at him and growled against the gag in her mouth, but Haggard tossed her to the ground like a child. He put his knee across her shoulders and waved the knife.

"You coming, boy, or do I get a new scalp-lock for my war shirt?"

I stood up and walked into the clearing.

"There you go, youngster," said Cletus, taking the tether rope from my hands. "You ain't as dumb as she said you was. Haw haw." He hit me hard in the ribs with his rifle butt.

"Don't bang him up too bad, Cletus," Haggard put in. "He's got to keep up with us."

"I thought you wanted to leave him for bear bait."

"Changed my mind."

Cletus sighed, and then he kicked my feet out from under me. At least he was halfhearted this time. I lay in the sand, thinking I would have to watch him better. He was like Joab, I figured: "Art thou in health, my brother?" and then stab you. And I wondered what Haggard had in mind now, not sure it would be any better than bear bait. At least it wouldn't happen right away. I tried to concentrate on Johnny's training and pushed the fear of getting hurt away from me. I looked over to where Rosalie lay on the ground. I'd never seen her so angry, and somehow I felt it was my fault.

"Did you do the squaw?" Haggard asked.

"Couldn't spot her," said Cletus. "Nor the other two, neither. All three of them must have went off somewheres."

Haggard changed from friendly to furious in a heartbeat. He spun around toward Cletus.

"You were supposed to find them and finish them! The ruckus with the bear was our only chance, and you let them get away!"

"We'll finish them afterward," Cletus answered slowly. "At least, if they're gone off now, they won't be following us." I could see his left hand stealing toward one of the many knife handles that stood out from his belt.

"You're a coward and a fool, McGee," spat Haggard. His eyes bulged. "I oughta cut out your yellow liver and make you eat it right now."

"I know, Tom, but you don't want to do that," said Cletus. He spoke carefully, as if he were talking to a dangerous child. "I'm the only partner you got now. If you do me in, there's nobody else who'll ride with you. You don't want to be all alone, Tom. If you cut me up, you'll be all alone."

Some of the tension went out of Haggard. He settled back on his heels and began to search the brush with his eyes. He shifted on his feet. When he looked at Cletus again, he was a changed man.

"Where'd you hide the horses, Cletus? We better move before Clements figures out these two lovebirds ain't just cooing in the brush somewhere."

Cletus laughed. "Haw haw! That's a fact, Tom." He yanked on Rosalie's tether and gave me a quick kick in the side. "Up you go, babies. You got a long walk ahead of you."

Three

We trotted southwest along the Oregon Road until the moon was straight overhead, and then we left it where it crossed a small stream. We walked southward in the water for an hour before we clambered out onto a flat shelf of limestone. My feet were numb from the icy water, and my legs were dead weight from the speed of the pace we'd been keeping.

It had been even harder on Rosalie, I could tell. At first, as soon as the men took our gags off us, she insulted Haggard and Cletus constantly, calling them things I'd never read in the Bible. As time went on, though, she wore down and took to pleading with them and crying. She'd been moaning about her shoes, and she'd fallen down on the trail several times. She'd torn her skirt in two places. Sometimes she clung to my arm and cried loudly till Haggard told her to shut up or he'd put the gag back in her mouth.

Rosalie and I sat panting on the limestone bank where Haggard left us—a place where we would leave no tracks.

Haggard scouted ahead for the trail he wanted to take, and Cletus handed each of us a twist of buffalo jerky.

"Tuck into this," he said. "It's all you get till sunup."

I reached for the jerky and Cletus dropped it on the rock. He chuckled.

"Stay right here, babies," he said. "If you run off, we'll just ride you down and drag you for an hour."

He took his horse back into the water and let him forage along the bank.

"Daniel," Rosalie whispered, "where do you think they're taking us?"

"No idea. But I don't think we'll like it."

"Can we get away?"

"Not yet," I said. "And if we did, where would we go?"

"You think Mr. Clyman and Johnny will come after us?"

I thought about this.

"Well," I said, "if they do, I'm not sure they can get to us in time."

"That's what I think, too," she said. "It's mostly up to us. But I've been marking the trail just in case, to make it easier for them."

I was suddenly angry with her, and I didn't know why.

"You've been doing what?"

"Marking the trail. You don't think I fall down that much because I'm a girl, do you?"

I looked away. Marking the trail. Why hadn't I thought of this? Here I was supposed to be the mountain man's son.

"Listen, Daniel," she continued, "these men are both crazy, and they think I'm just a weak child from St. Louis with a smart mouth. I intend to let them think that. Every time I feign exhaustion and fall down, they look forward and back along the trail. They're so worried about someone following us that they don't see me break a twig, or make a gouge or a scuff in the trail. Or leave a piece of my skirt." She paused. "Or something like this."

She moved her wet shoe slightly, so I could see that she'd been scrubbing a pebble with her heel against the surface of the limestone where we sat. She had scratched a straight bright mark with a loop at the top and a short tail: the letter "R." I just shook my head.

"How did you think of all this?"

"Don't forget I'm half and half," she said, smiling. "I know tricks from both sides. Anyway, I could track a frog through water when I was four years old. I only hope Johnny and Mr. Clyman are half as good, because I can't leave them a map."

"Here comes Haggard," I said.

Without looking up, Rosalie clutched my arm and threw her head against my shoulder.

"Oh, Daniel!" she moaned. "I'm so tired. Boo hoo hoo!" I almost laughed out loud.

"Get her ready to travel, boy," Haggard snapped. "You won't want me to do it, that's sure. I am sick to death of that city girl." He looked around for Cletus and whistled one piercing note.

We left the stream and followed a game trail out onto the eastern edge of a broad grassy valley or basin. From there, we turned due south and cut across country, following no trail that I could see, until the sun showed over the peaks to our left. Soon after that, Haggard pulled up by a small spring in an aspen grove, and we stopped.

Cletus dropped more jerky in the dirt in front of us.

"There you go, babies," he said. "And then you better get some sleep; there's another long walk coming this afternoon." He threw a worn-out trade blanket toward us and turned away.

Rosalie put on her very sweetest voice.

"Mr. . . . um . . . Mr. Tom?" she said to Haggard. "Excuse me, but could I ask you a question?"

Haggard didn't know how to act.

"Huh?" he said. "My name is Tom, not Mr. Tom. Or, no, it's Mr. Haggard, to you. Mr. Haggard—ain't that right, Cletus?"

"Right as rain, Mr. Haggard, sir," replied Cletus with a smirk.

"Well," Rosalie went on, "Mr. Haggard, I was just thinking that, while we're resting, I could mix up some biscuits for everyone. Daniel will attest that my biscuits are among the best he's ever eaten. Won't you, Daniel?" She elbowed me in the ribs.

"Forget it, white girl," Haggard sneered. "This ain't no tea party. I don't want you making biscuits. I don't want you falling off a cliff gathering wood, and I don't want you setting fire to the whole damn country. I want you to eat that jerky and get some shut-eye, so you don't slow us down no more."

"But, Mr. Haggard . . ." Rosalie started. He cut her off.

"And I don't want no arguments," he snapped. "I swear, you talk as much as some of my sisters. Now you go lay down somewhere and stay out of Cletus's and my way. I can't stand city girls, and he likes them a little too much. Don't you, Cletus?"

"Mr. Haggard," said Cletus with a nasty grin, "white girls is my one and only weakness." They both chuckled, as Rosalie flushed and looked from one to the other.

"If my father, Angus McCulloch, were here . . ." she began through clenched teeth. I put my hand on her arm.

"Rosalie, why don't we find some shade and get a little sleep?"

"Don't touch me!" she flashed. Cletus and Haggard burst out laughing. She threw down her jerky and stalked away to the trees.

"Better get her to eat, boy," Haggard warned, suddenly very serious. "I ain't joking that I don't want her slowing us down."

"Yessir, I'll try," I said.

He clamped a chunk of jerky in his teeth and sliced it cleanly through with his scalp knife.

Four

CLETUS AND HAGGARD stood resting their horses
while Rosalie and I collapsed on the ground. My legs had
given up merely cramping and had become two knotted
stumps of pain. Rosalie's eyes were hollow from lack of
sleep, and her face was gaunt. She breathed in deep, rasp-
ing sighs. We both were marked with lumps and bruises,
courtesy of Cletus and his sweet-voiced punishments.

We had covered more ground in three days than the
wagon train would normally go in a week. We stopped
only for water and dried meat, and to sleep for a few hours
in short bursts of exhaustion.

Our direction had been steadily south and southwest,
and we pulled up now on a bluff overlooking a wide, bril-
liant river not far below. The hills around were bare bones,
but down near the river, bunchgrass was thick, and cottonwood trees gathered in large clusters.

"There she is," I heard Cletus say. "That old Seetskeedee
sure don't change much."

"It don't change, and you don't, neither," Haggard replied in a fierce whisper. "Cletus, you run your mouth about as much as that girl does. Now you done told them where we're at."

A pair of buffalo were trotting away about a hundred yards from us. I kept my eyes on them, as if I hadn't heard the men talking. But Haggard was right. I knew exactly where we were now.

Seetskeedee was another name Mr. Clyman had used for the Green River. I knew we had to cross it sometime if we kept on south and west, but I couldn't have known we'd reach it so soon. From here, if Rosalie and I could get free, we could follow the river back upstream to where it crossed the Oregon Road. Not far west of there was Fort Bridger. In the other direction, downstream and south more or less, lay a rough-looking range of snow-capped peaks. I thought they must be what Mr. Clyman called the Utah Mountains. They seemed to cut off any hope of passage, but I knew the river found a way through. Pa had told me you could follow the rivers from here all the way to the Gulf of California.

"They're greenhorns, Tom," Cletus replied in a soothing voice. "They don't know nothing." He turned to me. "Do you, boy?"

"Sir?" I said. "I'm sorry, I was watching the buffalo."

"See, Tom?" Cletus told him. "They're greenhorns. Sometimes you worry too much."

Haggard rolled his eyes and led his horse down off the bluff. Cletus followed, and so did we on our tethers.

"You know where we are?" Rosalie murmured under the noise of scuffling horse hooves.

"Green River," I whispered. She raised her eyebrows high and silently mouthed two words.

"Your father."

I nodded.

Cletus and Haggard had brought no pack mules with them, so I knew they had planned on a short trip from South Pass. I figured they had a camp of some sort waiting for them across the river, or maybe downstream.

The Green River was belly-deep on the horses where we crossed. The water was clear and cold as ice, and the men let their horses drink their fill, while Rosalie and I chewed on yet another ration of buffalo jerky.

Then we walked downstream along faint trails all afternoon, south toward the mountains.

The other thing I knew about this area was that it belonged to Mexico. The border with United States territory was somewhere north of Fort Bridger, which must be a few days upstream. But if the government of Mexico claimed the land, so did the Utes, and they seemed to be the ones truly in charge. According to my pa and Mr. Clyman, the Utes were a busy nation. Between here and Santa Fe, they laid out the best trade routes, knew the best hunting, knew all the languages around them. And they were excellent with horses—raising them, trading them, and stealing them. Spanish ranchers as far away as California had lost fine horses that showed up later in Taos, Santa Fe, or even Fort Bridger.

The sun was going down when we struck a well-used trail. Cletus and Haggard gave no sign, but the horses pricked up their ears and stepped out more eagerly, so I figured we were getting close to a permanent camp of some sort. About dark, we came over the shoulder of a low ridge and into what looked like a trading post.

Haggard reined his horse and looked the place over cautiously. A low square building made of logs hunkered down at the mouth of a small canyon that came in from the west. Gathered loosely around it were about a dozen well-worn tents and tepees. Cut brush and firewood were stacked here and there, alongside cooking fires, hide stretchers, tools, and racks for drying meat. Toward the rear, fir trees and aspen came down the slopes of the canyon to the banks of a rocky stream. Horses and mules were turned out to graze downhill from the camp. We could see a dozen men scattered here and there, tending fires, chopping wood, talking, eating, and drinking.

"Tom," Cletus chuckled, "you're home. Let's go on in."

Haggard still hesitated. "I just want to be sure he ain't here. Don't see his horses."

We moved down the ridge and into the camp. The men we passed called out to Cletus and Haggard.

"Well, if it ain't the prodigals come on home," one of them teased. "I thought you done give it up for life at the fort, Cletus."

"Once more for old time sake," Cletus said, and laughed. "Tom here finally made me a decent offer."

Behind the log building was a lean-to for storage. Haggard dragged out two wide rolls of canvas and assorted wooden poles, peeled and cut to size. He threw the canvas onto the horses and made Rosalie and me drag the poles a hundred yards up the hill, toward the trees.

"You get these tents put up," Cletus ordered as he untied our hands. "Me and Tom are going to socialize."

He dropped two more twists of jerky on the ground.

"Supper," he said as he moved to go. Then he turned back to us for a moment. "Oh, and I wouldn't even think about running off, if I was you. You can't get nowhere that we can't find you. And even if you could, the wolves would get you, anyway. They's wolves aplenty around here."

He led his horse away to graze with the others.

Rosalie rubbed her wrists furiously. "Why do they think we'll put up these tents for them?" she demanded when Cletus was out of range. "Why should we, after what they've put us through?"

"Because if we don't they'll beat us again and starve us."

"That is no answer, Daniel LeBlanc," she snapped. "I almost think you've caved in."

I sighed. "Rosalie, I'm just being practical. We both know that getting out of here will be hard enough; broken bones will only make it harder."

She thought about this, and then she began unrolling one of the tents.

"What do you think this place is?" she asked. "Who are the people here?"

"I think they're outlaws," I said. "I think they steal guns and horses and whiskey and anything else they can get from the wagon trains. They trade them to the Utes. And I think they trade a few slaves, too, like Mr. Clyman said."

Slaves. The word itself made me cold. There were slaves in the Bible. There were slaves in Missouri. I thought about Johnny. He was born a slave, and in most states he wouldn't be free today. But I had always believed what Aunt Judith said about that. Before our Maker, there is no slave, and there should be none in our country, either. After my forced march on a rope behind a horse; after living on dirty scraps of food; after being dragged, bossed, beaten, and threatened; near certain to be sold to the Utes right soon—after all this, I understood a little more about Johnny. The idea of slavery for a lifetime frightened me in my bones.

Rosalie and I finished with the tents, and then we cleared a small space for ourselves in a cluster of aspen and fir nearby. We pulled our ragged trade blanket over us and tried to sleep as the wolves called and night closed over the canyon.

Five

"Stop. Stop it." Rosalie's voice was in my ear. I dragged an eye open to see dawn just beginning to lighten the sky.

"Don't tickle."

I twisted my head to look. Rosalie was asleep on my shoulder, with one arm thrown across my chest, and she was talking in her sleep.

"Mmm. Don't tickle. Please," she said.

I had no idea. I was about to drift back to sleep when I felt it. Two very small hands pressed gently on my ankle. I flinched but then held still, not breathing and not looking. The small hands found a grip and climbed slowly toward my knee, while two small feet followed them carefully. Then one hand wobbled, slipped off, and a fat little belly landed on my shin. Gentle scrambling, a dry rustling noise, and the belly heaved itself over. A warm, round body no bigger than a puppy curled up, nose to tail, on the blanket between my knees.

"Rosalie," I whispered. "Look."

"Mmm?"

"Look at this. I don't want to move, in case it's a skunk or something."

Rosalie lifted herself on her elbow, carefully.

"Oh my quills," she said, as if that was a swear. Then she began to laugh, silently.

"Oh, Daniel, you've done it; I never really believed you would."

"What?" I demanded. "Would you just tell me what it is?"

"Shh. It's my quills," she murmured, still laughing. "It's the fretful porpentine. I just wish South Wind Woman were here to tell me what to do next."

"A porcupine? Oh, wonderful." I started to get up.

"Lie still, now," Rosalie commanded, "while I think what to do. He's just a little one. You must make a nice nest."

I strained for a better look. He was round; that was my first impression. His head was small, his tail was short, and in between was a chubby mound of brown fur and bright quills. And he looked far too comfortable between my knees.

"We don't have anything to kill him with," I said. "And he might stick me if we try."

"We're not going to kill him, you fool. Just lie still while I try something."

"Be careful."

"Shh."

Slowly, Rosalie raised one corner of the blanket and reached across me for another. She sat up carefully and gathered the other two corners. When she began to lift, the porcupine sensed what was up. He struggled and scrambled and threw himself toward freedom, and I got fourteen black-and-yellow quills down the inside of my left leg. Right through the blanket.

Rosalie had him off me in a second, and she laid him on the ground still thrashing. She whispered to him while she rolled him gently a few times. It was the funniest thing I'd ever seen. He was frantic to get away from the blanket, but every time he got his nose out, Rosalie was there to wrap him back up.

"Just a minute, my friend. Just let me have a few. *Ow!* I'll take good care with them. *Ow!* I'll take good care. You'll be—*ow!* You'll be pleased with me when I make something beautiful from them. *Ow!* Thank you, thank you, thank you."

She sat back finally and let the fellow find his own way out of the blanket. He waddled briskly away, his quills bristling like rays from a small brown sun, while Rosalie opened the blanket.

"Look!" she cried. "He must have left a hundred!"

"Here, you can add these to the collection." I passed her the handful I had picked out of my leg.

"I'm sorry," she said. "Did he get you badly?"

"Nah. I guess I won't bleed to death."

"Good. Now I have to pull these out of the blanket and get them in a bundle somehow. I can tear a strip from the blanket for that."

"Or we can steal a piece of buckskin around here," I suggested.

Rosalie was almost happy. I was already starting to fret about what new trouble today would bring, but she had found a way to put that out of her mind. Nothing like getting me stabbed a few times to cheer a girl up, I thought.

"The first thing I'll make is an amulet for South Wind Woman. Besides, Pickett's war shirt is back at the wagons."

She set herself to plucking the quills, and I moved quietly down toward the camp. Haggard was sleeping in one of the tents we had raised; I could hear him muttering in his dreams. Cletus was in the other, snoring through his ragged teeth. The men in camp had been awake late into the night, laughing and yelling; I had heard a shot fired once, and then more laughter.

The only person I saw awake now was a woman I thought might be a Ute. She had struck a small fire and was crushing something in a bowl beside one of the tepees near the log house. Several yards away, in about the center of the camp, was a wide fire pit ringed with stones. There was a sitting log and two upturned wooden stools, a few cups, and a whiskey jug, along with a pair of willow backrests near the fire. One of these was on its side. Nearby, a man lay on his back in an awkward position, his arms bent wrong and his head to the side. Blood was caked on his face and ear. I stopped by the woman and squatted down to speak to her.

"What happened to him?" I asked, nodding toward the man on the ground.

Her eyes flicked over there. She said something in a language I didn't know, and she shrugged. I made the hand sign for repeat.

"Dead," she told me. She glanced at him again.

"Who killed him?"

She looked at me sharply, as if I'd asked where the sun sets, and she drew one finger down her left cheek.

"Haggard," I murmured. "Should have guessed."

I wandered over toward the dead man. I knew I shouldn't be thinking this way, but it struck me that he might have a gun or a knife or something else that I could steal before the other men woke up. Judging by the tracks around him, though, the woman had already beat me to it. All I found was a small priming horn, which hung from a thong around his neck and had been trapped out of sight under a shoulder. I took it back to the woman.

"Trade?" I asked.

She looked it over. It was made from a piece of buffalo horn, small and scuffed. But it still held powder, and there were no splits along the base plug or stopper. She shrugged and made the sign for trade.

I nodded toward a skinning knife that lay on the ground. But, no, she wasn't interested in trading that. I hinted at an almost finished pair of moccasins; she waved her hands and shooed me away.

"What will you trade?" I asked. She shrugged again and waved me off. I gave up. "Well, I don't need this." I dropped the priming horn beside her and walked back up the hill.

"Nice try, though," Rosalie said. She had been watching everything. "And now you've given her a gift; maybe she'll repay us later."

Six

CLETUS THREW his saddle on the ground and sat while he directed us in setting up their camp. We dug a shallow fire pit and hauled rocks from the creek to ring it and to set pots on. We set a tripod over the fire and hung an iron kettle of beans to simmer. Haggard came by with a cut of elk, which Cletus sliced into the beans. They did any cutting that needed to be done, and never let us near a knife or any kind of weapon.

We built a lean-to beside the fire, and dragged more supplies from where Haggard had them stashed. We carried the two willow backrests from near the dead man and set them up for Cletus and Haggard. From here, they could watch the whole area.

In the afternoon, Cletus made us dig the grave. It was one of the few times I'd seen Cletus when he wasn't jolly.

"Who is he?" Rosalie asked.

"He *was* the booshway, the storekeeper for the boss. You keep digging."

"Why did he get killed?"

Cletus grunted. "Stupidity, mostly. Said the wrong thing to Tom Haggard when he was drinking."

"What did he say?"

"Look, it don't matter. You just tend to your digging."

Cletus looked up toward the canyon and blew out a long sigh.

"Hell, it don't matter a bit, truth to tell," he said. "Tom just had to kill somebody. He's been tighter than a war drum lately. When he gets that way, somebody's headed for the happy hunting ground, sure as the world. Happens every time." He spat on the ground. "Every damn time. Yep. And the boss ain't going to like it."

We dug awhile in silence as Cletus fell into a daydream.

"Who's the boss?" I asked finally. Cletus jumped.

"Will you two gabby outfits just clamp your traps before I have to smack you around?"

"Sorry."

Nobody spoke for a minute.

"Since you have to know so much," Cletus said in the same testy tone of voice, "the boss could put down Tom Haggard and any *two* other men in this camp with one hand tied behind him. He'd do it, too, even if Tom *is* his dead wife's brother."

Cletus snorted at some joke of his own.

"Heh, that's pretty good. One hand tied. The boss only has one hand anymore. Heh heh."

"Really?" Rosalie prompted.

"Sure enough," he said.

In spite of his mood, there was nothing Cletus liked better than telling tales.

"The boss got bit by a wolf last fall. A mad wolf. Big white lobo come out of the woods foaming at the mouth. He looked like a ghost on wheels, and there was nothing but death on his mind. Tore up two horses straight off, and then he killed a man in his bedroll. The boss was standing at the woodpile, and he was next in line. That lobo jumped him so fast, I couldn't believe he got his hand up in time. Wolf grabbed his hand and crushed it, but the boss brained him with a piece of firewood. That man was so strong, he probably killed the wolf with the first whack, but I think then the boss went a little mad himself. Just kept beating that wolf and beating him, till he wore out his good arm and we could drag him away."

We were quiet as Cletus went on, his voice low.

"He got the hydrophobies all right, but he managed to live through it. There was an old mountain-man healer around here, a strange old bird. Lived too long with the Cheyenne, I guess. And he told the boss to cut the arm off at the elbow. Said that would keep the sickness from reaching into him too far. His hand was worthless now, anyway. So that old man done it—popped it off at the elbow with a boning knife and then stitched up the stump with beaver gut. I never seen the like."

I shuddered, but Rosalie kept digging.

"Then what?" she asked. Cletus leaned into his tale.

"Well, then the old guy did some kind of witching stuff to him. To cure the sickness, he said. Wouldn't let nobody in the big house, and he kept the place full of steam and incense. Cooked a lot of funny stews. And he hung that white wolf hide by the door."

Cletus lowered his voice to almost a whisper now.

"But he hung the hide without the head, because he used it somehow. Some ceremony. We could hear him singing in there, calling up all kind of Indian devils and gods, and we could hear the boss moaning and raving from the sickness.

"We was all spooky as cats about it. Then Tom got drunk one night and said he couldn't stand no more of that mumbo jumbo. Went in himself to break it up. But, do you know, the boss threw him out with his one good arm, sick as he was. Threw him out the door like he was shot from a sling."

Cletus shook his head, his face flushed. His assorted knives, pistols, and pouches clung to him like a patchwork. He glanced over his shoulder toward the log house, where we could see the headless white wolf hide still hanging.

"Six weeks he was in there, and when he come out he looked like he'd been to the grave and back. His face was bone white from lack of sun. Half his weight was gone, but he was still tough as the wolf that bit him. Tougher. He showed us that as soon as he come out the door. Walked up to the first man he saw, and that was Big Bull Tremblais.

"Now, Bull was twice as wide as me and strong as any ox. He'd been saying we oughta pick ourselves a new chief. Said the boss couldn't do it no more after this. How the boss knew about that, we never could figure. But he took Bull by the throat in his one hand, picked him clean off the ground, and threw him down on his back so hard the breath went right out of him. He leant down and said real quiet-like, 'Now, Bull, are you going to be chief or am I?' Big Bull never said a word; he just gathered his kit and hit the trail."

Cletus raised an eyebrow, checking to be sure we got his point. Then he went on. "And the boss had lost his hair—that was the strangest thing. He always had a head of hair on him, thick and black and long to the shoulders. Lost it all in the sickness, and he looked ghostly without it. Bald like a skull. Fearsome. And when his hair grew back in, what do you think? It was white as the wolf, that's what!"

Rosalie and I had stopped digging long ago, and now Cletus gestured for us to get back at it.

"Then what?" Rosalie asked again.

"Well. Then the old healer disappeared. Some said he went back East. But the boss, he started doing the Indian magic his own self. Sweat-lodge stuff. Chanting in there all night long, sweating, howling even. He'd come out and his eyes would be different, like he'd seen the ghost of the wolf itself. And he'd say, 'The buffalo are moving up in the basin,' and we'd go look—forty miles away—and there would be buffalo by the thousand. Or he'd say, 'Fort up, there's a Ute party coming down the canyon.' And sure enough, we'd get ready, and here they'd come. Only they'd come in gentle as lambs, just to powwow with the boss. Somebody seen him in a dream, or somebody had a vision, and they're just bringing a gift to the White Wolf. To keep him from killing them all, I guess. He'd chant with them a night or two and off they'd go. Didn't even bother the horses."

Cletus stopped again to breathe. He fiddled with one of the charms tied up in his hair.

"Yep, it's been a touch on the eerie side around here. Makes me a little jumpy, and it sure makes Tom hard to get along with. But I wouldn't trade it. What I say, it's better to have a magic man looking out for you than hunting for you."

He bent down and grabbed the dead man by the front of his shirt with both hands. He dragged him to the edge of the grave and tumbled him in.

"There you go, greenhorns. Now, cover him up nice."

Seven

THE MEN were passing a whiskey jug around the fire. They were laughing and arguing, but they were quieter than the night before. And so far no shots had been fired. Haggard sat to one side, speaking to no one.

The Ute woman was by her tepee, and Rosalie thought we should try to talk to her while Cletus and Haggard were busy. She made the sign for greeting, and found out the woman's name was Gray Owl. Then she noticed the moccasins I had seen before. Gray Owl handed her one.

"Very strong," said Rosalie, testing the stitches. The woman nodded and took the moccasin back.

Rosalie unrolled the scrap of blanket that held her new porcupine quills. Gray Owl grinned. Something about the quills struck her funny. She picked up a few and inspected them. They were short, compared with the ones that South Wind Woman had been using, and Gray Owl made the sign for "young." Rosalie laughed.

"Yes." She nodded, holding her hand not far off the ground. "Just a little fellow."

The woman signed for us to wait, and she went into the tepee. She came back shortly with a small bladder pouch, very tough but pliable. She passed it over to Rosalie.

"Oh, thank you," said Rosalie. "That'll be much better." She fingered it open and spilled the quills into the bladder. Gray Owl stepped back into the tepee and came out with a man's buckskin shirt. Decorating each shoulder was a long rectangle of quill work—red, black, white, and yellow. I couldn't help noticing one sleeve was cut off at the elbow.

I stood up to stretch my legs while they talked. Women things, I thought. I wandered toward the front of the log building.

The low roof came down almost to my head height; most grown men would have had to duck under to get through the door. The logs were starting to split from harsh weather, and it looked like dry rot and insects had settled in to stay. The corner notches were badly fitted, and the ground underneath the building had shifted, slanting one corner down by half a log. This gave the whole thing a twisted look, as if the madness that went on inside had affected the outward appearance.

I came to the wolf skin tacked beside the door. He must have been longer than I was tall, with feet fully the width of my hand. If it had been cleaned and tanned properly, this would have been a valuable pelt. But even burying a mad wolf was more contact than most people would want; skinning him must have taken real courage, and treating the hide was out of the question. The fur was coarse, stiff, and dirty. The flesh side was starting to crack from the weather, and the shoulders, where the head had been taken off, were darkened by blood. I shuddered.

And then I heard a scream. Rosalie.

I stumbled toward the sound, moving as fast as I could in the near-darkness. I came around Gray Owl's tepee and saw Rosalie near the men's fire. The men were standing in a rough half-circle, their faces washed orange in the firelight, and in the center was Haggard. He had forced Rosalie to her knees, and he held her by the hair with one hand while he waved a burning stick in his other. She screamed again as Haggard touched her shoulder with the firebrand.

"You gotta remember who you belong to now, city girl!" he shouted drunkenly.

I threw myself into him. The firebrand skidded over the ground and Haggard went sprawling across Rosalie. He came up and I hit him as hard as I could, right on his crooked nose. He hardly seemed to notice.

I knew that now was the time to run, before Haggard beat me to death, but, strangely, I felt calm. I wasn't going to run. I wasn't going anywhere.

He had a fistful of my shirt in his left hand, and he smacked me with his open right. My head rang. Without thinking, I locked his fist on my shirt. Johnny's voice went through my mind. *Very nice for you, really—it keep his hands busy.* Haggard reared back for another swing. This time, I drove two fingers into the notch at the base of his throat. He choked and stumbled. I twisted right and hammered his elbow hard with my fist. He tried to pull away, but I had his hand trapped. I levered myself against his arm and stamped his left knee sideways. Haggard went down and I jumped on top of him.

That was my mistake. On the ground, the advantage was all his. Haggard trapped my leg beside him and rolled. I poked his eye and threw my knee into his secrets, but his weight turned me onto my back. He choked me with both hands, pounding my head against the ground. I pulled one of his thumbs and thought I broke it. I found a rock with one hand and I brained him. It didn't seem to matter; he kept choking me, leaning onto my throat. His eyes bulged, and his stringy hair swung back and forth above me like a nest of snakes.

My eyes fell on his wide belt and the knife that hung there in its sheath. I dragged it out and stabbed deep into his thigh. Again. Again. Haggard jerked away and rolled off me, holding his leg. I staggered up, not sure I could take a step. My throat burned. I couldn't breathe or focus my eyes. I turned, trying to find him.

He was turning, too, and in his hand was a wicked-looking pistol. I stood stock-still, as if I was trapped in one of my dreams. The firelight painted him orange and yellow, black and blood-red, all the colors of hell. How strangely beautiful it was, though I was certain I would die in two seconds. Haggard pulled the hammer back and raised the pistol slowly toward me. I'd never seen a hole as deep as the barrel of that gun.

"Haggard!" a voice boomed out. "Put it down."

Haggard wavered for one second, and then he fired. Before I even heard the shot, I felt the ball tug at my hair and whiz past into the night.

Just as quickly, the butt of a rifle reached out of the darkness and swept Haggard's legs out from under him. He landed hard and didn't move. A broad-shouldered man in buckskins stepped into the light. A strong man with ferocious eyes. His hair and beard were white as the moon, and one arm was cut off at the elbow. He stood for a moment looking down at Haggard.

"This man is finish," he said in the same deep voice, slightly colored with French. "Cletus, you pack his gear and get him on the horse. He is mad wolf now—if any man see him again, you kill him."

Then he swung slowly around the circle of men, pointing his rifle like a huge finger at each one of them in turn.

"And you are dead, too, if any man of you lay one hand on my son."

The rifle came to rest on me.

PART FIVE

Etienne

One

A BANK OF CANDLES flared on a small wooden table. Nearby, a fire glowed in a rough stone fireplace. Between the candles and the fireplace, Rosalie sat on a stool while Gray Owl worked on her shoulder. The burns had blistered into an ugly mass of dark bubbles, and Rosalie flinched as the older woman applied bear grease. Gray Owl chanted softly in a high voice.

The room was no more than twelve feet across, with the table built into the wall by the door and a low bunk built into the wall opposite, where I sat. To my left hung a curtain of dirty trade blankets tightly stitched together, cutting the room into a rough square. I didn't know what lay behind the curtain. On the floor by the curtain, animal hides—beaver, mink, marten—were baled and stacked among jumbled piles of traps and tools. A battered wooden trunk was pressed against one wall beside rumpled bags of beans, flour, tea, and other staples. Two heavy crates of brand-new rifles were stacked nearby.

The door swung open and my pa stepped in from the night. He said nothing, but leaned his rifle against the wall by the door and sat down in the center of the room, facing the fire. Gray Owl filled a bowl from a kettle of stew on the fire and handed it to him. Then she filled one for me. She finished binding Rosalie's arm and set a bowl for her on the table.

Pa was leaner than I'd ever seen him but still very broad, and there was a look of easy strength about the way he moved, like there is about a mountain lion. Or a wolf. It was a little frightening. He dressed simply, with none of the sashes, amulets, or charms that most of the other mountain men wore. There were no feathers tied in his hair. Down each shoulder was the only decoration he wore: a narrow strap of quill work in red, black, white, and yellow. He sat slurping his stew without a word. When he was finished, he spoke.

"You bring Haggard's tent and make the bivouac tonight by her tepee," my pa said to me. He nodded toward Gray Owl. "Tomorrow she feed you. You sleep. Eat. *Et puis,* you go."

Then you go. Simple as that. I couldn't quite take in the words. I didn't know how to answer.

"Cletus going to give you two horse and grub enough for three day. You and the girl, you go to Seetskeedee, and you follow upstream. Is an old trading post where the Road of Oregon cross the Seetskeedee. You leave those two horse there, and Cletus coming later to pick them up."

My head was spinning, and I felt like I might throw up. Very carefully, I set my bowl on the dirt floor.

"I'm not . . . I don't think I understand," I stammered.

"You cannot rest here, *mon ami*," he said more gently, but still commanding. "You are kidnap from the wagon company—this mean someone follow you right now."

"We don't know that."

"Is true," he said, nodding. "One old man come for you with two other. I see them in a dream."

"Mr. Clyman," whispered Rosalie. A look of hope spread across her face. Etienne glanced at her.

"*Oui*, Clyman." He smiled. "Back in the mountains, that old man. May he live one hundred year."

"Haggard wants to kill him," I said.

Etienne shook his head. "Never happen. Clyman, he outlive Haggard two time over."

I didn't believe it. But I didn't want to hear about Haggard.

"But why do I have to leave?" I asked. "I walked all the way from Missouri to find you. You can't just tell me to turn around and walk back."

"Daniel, don't be the child," he scolded. He jerked his head toward the crates of rifles impatiently. "What you think—I need these gun for hunting? No, I take them from the nice white men in the Fort Laramie. I trade them to the nice red men in the mountain. I am a pirate, Daniel, like in your schoolbooks. I have no place for boys and girls here.

"No," he murmured, looking away from me. "You go out to Seetskeedee, and you make the nice footprint for old Clyman to follow."

I stood up. My head was clear now, and I was angry. I wasn't about to be dismissed like a child.

"I won't do it!" I shouted. "I don't care about any of that. I've just walked a thousand miles because a voice in the night said you were in trouble. I've been told to turn around a hundred times. I've been shot at and cut and kidnapped and beaten and starved half to death, but I never gave up—and do you know why? Because you are the only real family I have in the world, and I knew you needed me. I knew it, Pa. And you will *not* send me away with a hearty meal, like some distant cousin who showed up for supper!"

I never saw him move. Suddenly my feet flew out from under me, and I hit the floor with a thump. He squeezed my jaw hard in his one hand, and he put his face down close to mine. His eyes glowed red in the firelight, and they drove into me.

"I do not permit one man in this camp to contradict me, and you no different," he said in a tone like death itself. "I know all about the voice in the night, *mon ami,* but this not *my* voice. I did not call you to come here, and you will leave because I wish it. And please don't tell me your trouble—I do not care. Those are *your* trouble." He let that sink in before going on. "I have watch you come here with Haggard, and I have see you and the girl very secretly mark the way. This make me proud of you. But you have make a trail that going to bring my enemies to my door." His fingers tightened around my jaw, and he shook my face slightly.

"Now, you rest one day, and you leave in the morning after tomorrow. And you lead Mr. James Clyman, and his shape-changing friend, and the woman of the wind, away from here."

I lay quietly, growing cold, pinned by his eyes. How could he know them like that? Compared with this moment, I had never been afraid before.

"*Et puis,* you are going to forget the way back," he warned softly. "For, if you do not, Daniel my son, I hang you from a tree by the ankle *moi-même,* and then I am calling the wolves to pull you down in pieces." He held my face one moment longer and then he let me go.

If he wanted to frighten me, he had done it. But I was angry, too. The miles I had come unrolled in my mind. I had walked each aching step like it was a gift for this man, for my father, and now he had thrown them all back in my face. My stomach was in knots. I could hardly think. But I was sure of one thing: I had come looking for my father but found a man I didn't even know. I had never been so shocked or so angry. Suddenly I hated him. I stood up and brushed myself off.

"I should have listened to Aunt Judith," I said hotly. "She knew you didn't care a damn about anyone but yourself. All my life, you've been gone from me more than you've been home. Gone to the river, gone to the mountains. Gone on the day my mother died. Well, I will tell you something, Etienne LeBlanc, this is the *last* time you'll ever desert me." I spat on the floor. "You're no kin of mine. I'm *not* your son. At least I can see that now."

He laughed out loud. A booming, musical laugh that filled the room and nearly knocked me down again.

"Mais, si! Absolument!" he roared. "You are my true son, yes. You have no idea, *mon cher*, how much you are my son." His face was creased with joy, and in it I saw him as he was so many years before. He turned to Rosalie and Gray Owl, tears of laughter streaming from his eyes. "It is to laugh! This boy, Daniel, he is walk a thousand mile to tell me so fierce that he's no my son—now *there* is the son of Etienne LeBlanc!"

I turned and stalked out, his laughter pealing through the night air behind me.

Two

I SLEPT FITFULLY, flinching at every sound in the night. My back and arms ached from the fight with Haggard. My knuckles and elbows were scraped bloody, there was a kink in my windpipe and a dozen lumps on the back of my head. Worst of all, every time I turned over, I could hear my father's words: *I do not care. I have no place for boys and girls.*

The sun was high and the tent was hot when I finally woke. Rosalie was sitting with Gray Owl by her tepee, stitching quills to a small circle of buckskin. She held it up.

"Look." She smiled. "For South Wind Woman."

I nodded. "How's your shoulder?"

"Hurts," she said. "But she made me some kind of tea for it. Willow bark, I think."

I looked around and saw Cletus coming up the hill toward us. I couldn't read his face.

"The boss says you greenhorns go back tomorrow morning. I'll bring a pair of horses up tonight and tie them in the trees there."

"We're not greenhorns," I said stiffly. He squinted, looking off toward the log house.

"Well, you can fight," he said. "I'll give you that. Never saw Tom Haggard get the worst of it before."

I shrugged. "I thought he'd kill me."

"He might yet."

"What? He's supposed to be gone."

"Tom's a mess," Cletus said flatly. "His head's cracked, his elbow's bent four ways from Sunday, and his leg's cut up real bad. But don't you think he's gone, boy. Don't you think he's dead until you see the body. He's in every shadow you'll ever see, and don't you never think he's forgot you."

Cletus dropped a pair of saddlebags by the tepee for Gray Owl to fill with food, and he sketched a rough map in the dirt to be sure we knew the way to the Green River. Then he turned and walked away without another word.

We had brought nothing with us but our clothes, so there was nothing for Rosalie and me to get ready. I pulled the dirty buffalo robe that belonged to Haggard from the tent and took it to Gray Owl.

"Trade?" I asked.

She judged the robe, and then she laid a short bow and a handful of newly feathered arrows beside it. I shook my head.

"Nah. I'm no good with them," I said.

She pulled out a little gun that had belonged to the dead booshway. It was a small duck-foot pistol, battered but well oiled. A shopkeeper's gun, with two hammers, two triggers, and two short barrels that separated slightly, like fingers making a V.

I hesitated. It wasn't a flintlock pistol; it needed the new brass percussion caps to fire. I had heard of these, but had little idea how to use them and nowhere to get them. I shook my head.

Gray Owl produced a small powder horn, along with a bullet pouch and a bright tin of the percussion caps. Still, I wasn't sure.

"What's the matter?" asked Rosalie.

"I don't know," I said. "It won't have much range, and I really like a flint better. Maybe I can trade this buffalo robe to one of the men for an old rifle."

"I'll use the pistol," Rosalie said quickly.

"You will?"

"Yes. I decided last night that the next time a man tries to drag me anywhere I'll have to put a hole in him. It's the only thing they understand." Rosalie made some hand signs, and Gray Owl smiled.

Eagerly she pushed the little gun toward Rosalie, along with the pouch and horn. Then she began piling other things beside them: a patch knife, a skinning knife, a flint and steel for fire starting, a small bundle of willow bark for making the tea for Rosalie's burn. Last, she handed Rosalie a small roll of leather tied with a single thong.

"Quills!" Rosalie whispered, unrolling the bundle. They lay across her palm, three inches long, black-tipped, some white, some black, some red, and some yellow. Rosalie beamed.

I still needed a rifle, and I felt a stronger need for it as the afternoon turned to evening. I tried to trade the tent that belonged to Haggard for a rifle, but none of the men were willing to have it.

I went up to the house and stood at the door for a long minute. We hadn't seen Etienne since last night. I figured he had gone out somewhere, looking for Mr. Clyman or meeting some of his Ute customers. I stepped in and closed the door behind me.

Darkness was almost total. The fire had burned down to embers under a light layer of ash, but the air was thick with steam and the smoke of incense. I found a candle on the table and lighted it with a coal from the fire.

Everything seemed in order, about as it was when I left the night before. I turned to the crates by the wall and lifted the lid from the top one. Six new Hawken rifles, made in St. Louis. They were shorter than the eastern hunting rifles, and they had sturdy maple half-stocks, perfect for the hard use they would get in the Rocky Mountains.

"Good idea, Daniel." Etienne's voice. I whirled to face him, but he wasn't there. "*Très bonne idée.* You take one, and take my pouch there, too. I have another."

His voice was tired, not the booming voice of command I had heard last night.

"Back here," he called. "Back here, through the curtain."

I pushed past the rough curtain and stepped into a wall of heat and steam. I began to cough.

"Get down," he said quietly. "Stay close to the floor."

In the center of the small room was a pit, dug directly into the dirt floor of the cabin. Within the pit was a pile of stones, each about the size of a fist. A bucket and a dipper stood nearby. The stones were slick with heat, and steam rose from them in a slow cloud. Etienne slouched, naked, against the back wall of the room. Through the steam I could see that his white hair was drenched and his body running with sweat.

"You never been to sweat before?" he asked, strangely.

"Heard of it," I said. I didn't like how distant and weak his voice had become. "Are you all right?"

"*Très bien, mon cher.*"

"Why are you doing it?" I started to cough again.

"It is to purify," he said. "I sweat away this world so to enter the other one. You try it sometime. You dream dreams like in the buffalo circle."

"So that *was* you," I said in a small voice.

He nodded. "You call me pretty strong that time. Surprise me."

I was silent for a moment.

"Why don't you come back with me?" I asked. "We can build a cabin. We can hunt. We can farm with Uncle John."

He sighed and looked away. My candle flickered in the small room, lighting one side of his face but leaving the other side in deep shadow.

"I don't speak of my mind to any man, Daniel, but I tell you this because you are my son," he said, some of the life returning to his voice. "I detest the white man, *mon cher*. *Je déteste* his wagon and his road and his fort and his farm. I hate how he tear the earth for gold, how he use up the animal like so much to throw away."

He sat up straighter, and the words came out strong and hard. "The white man, he come from the East with his churches and his soldier and his sickness. He pave the ground with the cobblestone until not one tree is standing. He do all this. But most of all, he starting to kill the Indian, just as in the East he has done.

"He kill them with the smallpox. Your Mandan girl— she very lucky. In her country, eight thousand Indian die from the smallpox. Think of that, *mon cher,* eight thousand Mandan, Blackfeet, Assiniboine dead in two month time. Some gone crazy from the pain and fever and stink, some half eaten by the maggot before even they die. All this from the white-man disease.

"He kill them with the gun, too. I myself have seen how he shoot the Indian for sport, Daniel. For games. I have seen the villages burned, the women shot, the babies tossed in the river. Yes, he kill them with the gun. He killing also the buffalo they eat, to starve them, to make them the beggar, just as he did in the East. Who does this? The white man, the white man." He paused to breathe.

"Daniel, before I am born, the white president say the land never to be taken from the Indian, but I see with my own eyes how the government keep that promise. They going to march the Indian away from home and leave them in the desert. Just as in the East."

Etienne sighed. I felt his deep sadness.

"So is that why you trade rifles to the Utes?"

"*Oui, absolument.* I trade rifles to the Utes. I trade them also to the Cheyenne, the Crow, the Sioux, and Shoshone. This will not save them, but I do it."

I sat quiet, trying to take in what he was saying. This was not what they taught me in school. The West was supposed to be a vast wilderness, empty and barren and ready to be tamed. It wasn't supposed to be full of people already, women and babies, towns and villages.

"These thing are true, Daniel. In my dreams I am seeing the white man shoot the Indian from horses and from the locomotive. He going to kill them not just in ones and twos, but whole tribes. Not villages only, but nations. You see this in the medicine circle, no? You going to see this with your eyes. From Missouri to Oregon, same as from Boston to Independence."

"Why are they so important to you?" I asked. "I mean, I'm your *family.* How can you choose them over me?"

"Daniel," he scolded. "Open your eyes. Who do you think Gray Owl is?"

"Oh," I said. I started to get up.

"Sit down, *mon cher.* Your *maman* is safe in heaven these ten year." He leaned back against the wall. "You don't think your family is the only family, Daniel. Somewhere a Ute boy is learning to ride a horse. Somewhere a Lakota woman is meeting her man in the darkness. A Mandan girl miss her white father. You think these family should die so you can farm?"

"No, of course not," I said.

"You wish to farm, it is good to stay in Missouri. *Moi*, I wish to help the red man."

"But, Pa, you're a white man, too. Even your name is LeBlanc."

He smiled sadly.

"*Oui*, LeBlanc. But I think I am not so much white man since a long time, Daniel. I think I am *un homme perdu*. A lost man." His voice went quieter. "Now I am LeBlanc, the White Wolf of the mountain."

He was my father, but he spoke like someone I could never know. Could he have turned so completely against his own kind?

And where did I fit, then? I was white, too. I loved my farm and family as Aunt Judith did, and how I missed her right now. But I was also LeBlanc, like him. I sensed that he was right about the whites, because I saw it in Caldwell and Independence, in Fort Laramie and all through the wagon train. It was the same madness in the trapping companies, in Reverend Parker. The eagerness to subdue, to own, to use things up, and to kill. Would we kill them all? I thought of Gray Owl and South Wind Woman. I thought of Rosalie's mother and her village. And Rosalie. It wasn't hard to know my heart.

Maybe I could stop it or slow it down. Was that the way—stand against the wind as I had walked against it? I began to feel I had to try. Sweat trickled down into my eyes and down the middle of my back. I felt the thick hot air in my lungs like it was cleansing me from the inside.

"Pa, I have to ask you something."

"Oui, mon ami?"

"The Voice who called me. Wasn't that you?"

Etienne shifted in his seat against the wall.

"It is not easy to say," he murmured. "I did not come to you. That was the old man—the healer. We did not speak of you, but I think he know my heart about you. It may be I call you through the old man. Yes, I think maybe so."

"I knew it."

"You must trust what you know. But listen, *mon cher.* I watch you coming, and I learn something. I was maybe wrong to call you here. Last night, I try to tell you, but I get all mixed up." He sighed.

"I would have come twice this far," I said.

"Yes, but . . . how to say this to my son?" He stopped and spilled a dipper of water over the hot stones, sending another small geyser into the air between us.

"Daniel, your mother, she was my very soul. When I lose her, I lose my way complete. For some long time now I am more searching among the spirits to find her than I am out among the living. I thought maybe to bring you here was to bring her to me. And me back to the world. But no. That is not the way for me . . . and is not the path for you."

"I don't know about any of that, Pa. I just know I came because I wanted to find you."

"I know. I know. But you see, *mon cher*, I am not to find your mother, and you are not to find me. Maybe in this world we never do find the other, but listen: is much better you find yourself. That you can do. That you can do."

I had nothing to say. My chest ached from the steam and from loneliness. If I was never to know my father sitting in front of me, how was I ever to know myself? If this was not my path, then where?

"Daniel, I going to tell you something else very difficult. I think I going to die very soon."

"You mean they'll catch you?"

"The soldiers? *Non.*" He shifted his feet. "My trouble is Haggard, and he is your trouble, too, I think."

"What do you mean?"

"Haggard will come for me. His sickness will make him do it."

"Why did you let him get away, if you knew that?"

Etienne shook his head.

"I cannot kill the man, and he know it."

"Why can't you? You must have killed other men."

"Because, *mon cher*, I loved your mother," he whispered. "She was the sun and the moon to me, the angel of my soul." Etienne looked ghostly through the steam. His eyes met mine. "And this *farouche*, this wild demon Haggard, he is her brother."

Three

MY UNCLE. I sat by the tent wiping the new Hawken rifle with a rag. I knew that my mother and Aunt Judith had a brother. The twin who'd got in trouble with the law and had to leave the country. And I knew his name was Tom. But the last name was wrong, so I never put Haggard together with their long-lost brother. My uncle. I tipped powder from the horn and started a patch and a ball into the new barrel. He must not have known, either. He couldn't have tried to scalp his own nephew. He couldn't have stolen his own nephew for the slave trade, if he'd known. Could he? I rammed the load down.

"Daniel?" Rosalie sat down beside me. "Are you all right?"

"My uncle," I whispered.

"I know."

"How did you know?"

"I always thought you looked related. Something in your build, remember? It was nothing, really, at first. Just an impression. But then with what Cletus said . . ." Her voice trailed off. We heard an owl calling, somewhere in the trees beyond the log house.

"What did Cletus say?" I asked.

"Well, he said that Tom Haggard was the brother of the boss's dead wife. Remember? His brother-in-law."

"Yes."

"So then I knew."

"But you didn't know the boss was my father."

"Sure I did." Rosalie was her practical self. "From the minute you told me we were at the Green River, I knew that we would find your father. I just felt it. When we got here, no one else was the right man, and he was the only one missing. So I knew it had to be him."

The darkness crept down through the canyon, and it was settling around us now. A small cooking fire showed in front of a camp down the hill, casting wild shadows against a tent nearby.

"I'm scared, Rosalie," I murmured. "My uncle wants to kill me, and my father won't stop him."

Rosalie put her hand on the back of my neck and pulled my head gently down to her shoulder. I heard the owl in the trees again, closer this time. Rosalie's cheek was warm against my forehead.

"You'll stop him yourself, Daniel LeBlanc," she whispered. "You've done it before."

Four

"**G**ET UP, BOY!"

Swirling darkness. Flares of fire and lightning. A hand on my shoulder.

"Come, my friend; it's time!"

I was torn between dream and dream. I rolled over and pressed my forehead into the bedroll. Rain poured down in buckets. The sun scorched me. Dust, smoke, and steam. Buffalo thundered by, churning the world into mud, and a porcupine waddled off into the woods. Tepees went up in flames. White men were shooting, and Indians fell from their stolen horses. Utes and Blackfeet, Crows and Shoshones. A snake in a crown. Then my father stood before me, his eyes glowing brightly and his white hair flaming in the breeze.

"Get up, *mon ami*!" he said. "The serpent has stung me, and now he comes for you."

"Yessir, I will," I answered. "First thing."

"Daniel, wake up, my friend!" The hand was shaking my shoulder. "Daniel!"

It was Johnny.

"Let's go, my friend," he urged. "The time is now."

"Johnny?" I couldn't clear my mind. "Where's Etienne? He just told me . . ." From somewhere outside, I heard a shot. I leapt up.

"That's the way," said Johnny. "Now we go."

"No," I said, grabbing the new rifle. "It's Etienne. My dream." I pushed past him and out of the tent.

I rounded the tepee on a dead run and headed toward the log house through the dark. The door hung open, and the fire in the hearth burned brightly. Too brightly. Flames were climbing the rear wall and spreading toward the cot across from the door.

I could just make out a horse stamping nervously in the trees by the rear corner of the house. Haggard's horse. It fidgeted sideways, and then I saw him. He looked small. His face was pale; his eyes dark and hollow. Instead of a hat, he wore a red bandage wrapped around his forehead. He hung from the saddle with both hands, trying to get one foot in the stirrup and swing his bad leg over the horse's back. Blood soaked his leggings.

"Haggard!" I screamed. And then he was aboard the horse. I screamed again, and he turned, searching for me in the dark as he yanked the horse around. He saw me and grinned crazily, a huge knife clamped in his teeth. The scar on his cheek stood out like a bolt of lightning.

"Tom! Tom!" It was Cletus, limping into the light of the burning house. "Tom, wait! I got the girl for you!"

I froze, with the rifle halfway to my shoulder.

Cletus was staggering, but moving quickly. "I got the girl, Tom!" He panted.

One of Gray Owl's arrows hung from him. It had missed any vital points and had stuck in the thickest part of his beer-barrel chest. It flopped sickeningly. Another arrow ran through his thigh from back to front. Cletus held his rifle in his left hand, and his right arm was wrapped around Rosalie's neck.

"Tom!" he called again. "Wait for me!"

Then Cletus saw me, and he stopped. He looked at Haggard and then back at me.

"I'd put down the gun there, boy," he said with a chuckle. "You're outnumbered now. Besides"—he shifted his arm so that Rosalie's face was visible—"you wouldn't want the girl to get hurt, would you?"

Strangely, Rosalie smiled at me. Silently she mouthed one word: "Talk!"

"You let her go, Cletus," I said lamely. "This here's a brand-new Hawken rifle, and I can take off your head at this distance. You know I can."

Cletus shifted on his feet, and then he winced as his weight came down on his pierced thigh. I could see Rosalie fumbling with something in her skirt.

"We don't have even a minute for bluffing, boy," Cletus threatened. "You can't shoot me and Tom both with that thing, so put it down or I'll snap this city girl's neck right in front of you."

There was a muffled pop, and Cletus stood up very straight. He looked at me with a question in his eyes. Then a second pop, and the question disappeared. His eyes rolled back in his head and his legs folded up. Rosalie twisted away as he fell. The little duck-foot pistol was still smoking in her hand.

I rolled to one side as Haggard lunged the horse into me. He skidded to a stop and reined around for another charge, and I came up on one knee with the new rifle at my shoulder. The big knife was in his hand now. He raised it high as the horse pounded toward me again. I fired.

The knife went wild as the horse spooked at the gunshot. It reared, knocked me flat, veered around, and ran straight down the hill. I heard it crash through somebody's tent twenty yards away, and I caught a glimpse of Haggard as the horse blasted through a cooking fire. It was like a picture from a ghost story.

He had lost the reins, fallen forward, and wrapped both arms around the horse's neck. His bad leg flopped wildly, drenched in blood, but he clung to the saddle with his good one. Fresh blood blossomed on the back of his war shirt where my bullet had come out behind his shoulder. The horse stumbled, caught itself, and jumped a fallen log. I saw that much against the orange flare of firelight, and then he was gone.

Five

Johnny and Mr. Clyman were beside me.

"You lay still a minute," Mr. Clyman ordered, "and let's check for broken parts. That horse walloped you a good one. Then let's move back, before the fire has the house down on us."

"I think Etienne's still in the house," I said hoarsely, scrambling up.

"Alive, you mean?"

"I don't know, but we have to get him out."

Mr. Clyman turned to look at the fire. It had spread to the roof now, and most of the south end was in flames.

"You know where he'd be?"

"I think so," I said.

Mr. Clyman tore a wide strip from the hem of his shirt and began to tie it around his face. "Johnny, get a rope from the mule, would you?" he said.

"I'm coming, too," I said, jerking at my own shirt.

"I figured you'd say that."

"You don't know where he is," I said.

Johnny came back with the rope, making a loop as he ran. "Here's water, too," he said, dropping a gourd between us. "Cletus won't need it anymore."

"Where's Rosalie?" I wanted to know.

Mr. Clyman snorted. "Reloading, I expect."

He splashed my kerchief with water and then his own.

"Rosalie's good," Johnny explained rapidly. "She with the red mule and South Wind Woman." He handed me the loop. "You put this around him. Yank hard when you ready."

I ran for the door, with Mr. Clyman right behind me. The bunk and the wall near the fireplace were flaming, smoking, and popping, and the fire was beginning to over-take the rafters. Embers and smoke filled the air. We doubled over, keeping low where the smoke was lighter. Something fell in front of me, and I kicked it away toward the fireplace. I turned to Mr. Clyman.

"Rifles!" I shouted, pointing to the crates beside the wall.

"Damn!" He grabbed a short keg of powder and rolled it to the door, where Johnny snatched it from him. Then he took the handles of the rifle crates and dragged them out of danger, too, while I was struggling with the blanket curtain. Somehow, I couldn't find the end of it in all the smoke. The heat pressed around me like a huge fist. I began to cough and choke. Mr. Clyman put his hand on my arm.

"Daniel, stay low to breathe!" he reminded me. Then he snapped a knife handle into my palm. I knelt down and took a wet breath through my mask, then I reached as high as I could with the knife. I jabbed it into the blanket and sawed downward with all my might. Suddenly I was through the curtain and into the sweat room.

My pa lay as still as death on the floor by the pit. A buffalo robe, long and full and trimmed with ermine and eagle feathers, wrapped him from toes to chin, leaving only his face visible. His face was painted white, and covered with marks in red and black. Not broad stripes or lightning bolts, like war paint; these marks were small, even delicate. They looked like animal tracks, or letters, but not from any alphabet I knew. They covered his cheeks and forehead in a dense map of unreadable words. His cheeks and his forehead, and the rest of his head, too. He had shaved off his hair.

I crawled over to him.

"Pa!" I shouted in his ear. "Pa! Come on!"

He didn't move. His face was cold, and I couldn't feel a pulse in his throat.

Mr. Clyman was behind me. "Let's get this rope around him. We'll pull him out nice and gentle on his robe there."

We slipped the loop around his shoulders and sent a strong yank out to Johnny. With Johnny pulling steady on the other end, Mr. Clyman and I guided Pa over the floor, through the blanket curtain, and out into the smoke. The house was a fiery furnace now. There was a hole in the roof, and the flames were shooting through it, urged on by the draft coming in at the open door. The rafters were nearly burned through, and pieces of the roof were falling all around us. We dragged Pa through the rubble and out the door just as two rafters gave way and the whole south end of the roof crashed down in a whoosh of flame and smoke.

Six

SOUTH WIND WOMAN pushed the water gourd at Mr. Clyman. His hair was singed across the back of his head, and his face was streaked with soot. I was sure I looked about the same as I squatted by my father, coughing and coughing.

Rosalie knelt beside me and looked at his face, his shaved head. Gray Owl stood over us a moment, then she sat down a few yards away and began to chant quietly in her high voice.

"Is he hurt somewhere?" Rosalie asked. "I can't see it if he is."

"Here in the center." Johnny pointed to a neat bullet hole in the robe just above Etienne's crossed arms. "But no blood."

"No blood at all? Can you tell if he's breathing, Johnny?" asked Mr. Clyman.

"Yes, but very shallow, very slow breathing. His heart going too slow to make pulse much."

"We better open this robe," I said hoarsely. "See how bad he's hurt."

"You wait a moment," Johnny cautioned. "He not really here. This man, I think he be traveling."

Rosalie got it before I did. "You mean Haggard shot him while he was in a trance?"

"All dressed up for traveling," Johnny murmured. "Face all paint up for the spirits to read. Special robe. Sometimes men with great magic do it that way. So—the spirit be traveling, and old Haggard slide in like a snake to the nest."

"That's what he said in my dream," I whispered. *"The serpent has stung me."* I sat back on my heels. There were so many things I knew but didn't know. So many things coming to me from far away, and I didn't think I understood them. I felt the wind passing through me, like it did in the buffalo circle, like it did the first day I saw the mountains. I shuddered.

Johnny was watching me, and then he turned quickly to look over his shoulder.

"An owl, Johnny," said Mr. Clyman.

"Look, he's breathing," Rosalie said. "He's coming around!"

"Pa!" I shouted.

Slowly, his eyes opened. He seemed unsurprised, as if he knew we would be there. He looked from one of us to the next. His eyes rested on Johnny for a moment, studied him. Then he glanced at Gray Owl, who had stopped her chanting and stood at his feet now. He nodded. He looked at me last, and I felt his eyes probing me, as always.

"Daniel," he whispered.

The front of the buffalo robe lifted and he slid his hand toward me. I grasped it in mine.

"Pa, you can make it," I said. "Johnny can fix you up."

He closed his eyes and squeezed my hand. Something flat and round pressed into my palm, and then he smiled.

"From your mother," he said.

He took his hand away and closed the robe over himself again. A deep groan escaped him. In a moment, the blood began to well up from the hole in his chest, and then to flood. We could do nothing to stop it.

Seven

I DON'T KNOW what Aunt Judith would say, but I've come to think the human soul is a lonely and silent thing. Etienne did not belong to any of us. He was right to call himself a lost man, and we weren't sure that morning how he would want us to send him on his way. Gray Owl knelt near his body, her eyes closed and her head thrown back, calling, searching the darkness with her high voice. My father's wife. His widow. What would she do now? I wondered.

I felt lost myself. For what seemed years now, my pa had been like a destination for me. The walk from Missouri stretched behind me a thousand miles, and this was the first time I had not known which way to turn. He was lost to me, in spite of everything, but was I more alone now than before? I didn't know. Somehow I would find the path, and I knew he would want me to make the choice my own.

We sat in a circle around Etienne's body as the sun rose, filling the camp and the mouth of the canyon with light.

A Ute woman, an old white mountain man, an Oglala woman, a freed colored man, a girl half white and half Mandan, and me. Each of us needed some kind of ceremony for this moment, but we didn't know what to do.

South Wind Woman had been cutting food near the tepee. Now she handed Mr. Clyman a bowl and gestured for him to eat. He took something from it and passed it to Gray Owl. She passed it to Johnny. The bowl was filled with meat—elk and buffalo—cut in small pieces. It was cold but tender, and we ate the pieces silently. We passed it around the circle twice, with South Wind Woman urging us to eat until it was empty. Then she gave Mr. Clyman another bowl, this one filled with berries and some kind of root, chopped in small pieces. We finished that, too. Finally, she sent a water gourd around the circle, making sure that each of us got something to drink. We were all quiet for a moment, then South Wind Woman stood.

"*Mi takuye oyasin,*" she declared. "*Mi takuye oyasin.*"

Mr. Clyman nodded. Johnny smiled.

"All my relatives," he said. "Yes, we all family now."

We rose to our feet. Somehow the sadness and the lost feeling were lighter. Gray Owl turned to me and took my hand in hers. It was a gentle clasp, not like the hearty handshakes of men in church. Gentle, as if she'd slipped a feather from her hand to mine. Or a prayer. She did this with each of us in turn. We began to smile.

South Wind Woman and Mr. Clyman made a stretcher from long poles and tent canvas, and we lifted Etienne's body onto it and tied him securely. Carrying him, we followed Gray Owl out of camp along a narrow game trail. We left the mouth of the canyon behind, and walked over a low ridge where a broad slope of aspens spread out toward the north. Their leaves shimmered in the morning sun and made small whispering noises as we passed.

She led us to an open space where four aspens grew quite close together. Someone—I thought it must have been Etienne—had built a small platform in these trees not long ago. Gray Owl made us put the stretcher on the ground and step back. She began to chant again, very quietly, and then she unrolled something from her pack.

It was the skin of a wolf. From head to tail, it was longer than she was tall, and it draped loosely across her arms as she held it up. The hide had been tanned beautifully and groomed till the fur shone. The white fur.

Still chanting, she offered the wolf to each of the four winds, and then she spread it gently over Etienne. She motioned for us to raise him to the platform.

We left him there.

Eight

THE STOLEN HORSES were waiting in the trees where Cletus had left them. It took only minutes to saddle them and tie on our few possessions. Rosalie and I made our goodbyes to Gray Owl. Then we mounted and followed Mr. Clyman and Johnny on their horses, and South Wind Woman riding the red mule, back to the Green River and north to the Oregon Road. I stopped to look back only once.

The five of us met our wagon train at Fort Bridger, and Mr. Clyman went on with it to Oregon. Johnny decided to go with South Wind Woman back to her family. Rosalie and I rode with them as far as Fort Laramie where we waited until late October, when a small troop of soldiers on a survey mission passed through on its return trip to the East.

We traveled with the soldiers to Council Bluffs on the Missouri River, where we sold our horses and caught one of the last steamboats of the season heading south. We rode it down to Independence, and found ourselves on foot once again.

It was a brisk day in late December when we walked up the hill to Aunt Judith and Uncle John's cabin. There was a nip of more than frost in the air, and tiny snowflakes danced along the breeze. A drift of woodsmoke trailed from the chimney.

I hallooed the house as we came closer, and in a moment the door swung open. Uncle John stepped out, carrying his hat. He waved, took a pace or two toward us, and then he stopped dead in his tracks.

"Judith! You better come on out here," he called. "You won't believe me if I tell you."

Aunt Judith pushed past him. She wore her most skeptical look, and in one arm she cradled a bundle wrapped in a blanket. She stood by the door for one long moment, watching Rosalie and me climb the path. Then she handed her bundle carefully to Uncle John and came running.

She kissed me hard on both cheeks, and she banged me in the chest with her fist.

"I swear, Daniel LeBlanc, I have never been so glad to see a greasy old mountain man in all my life!" Then she turned and threw her arms around Rosalie.

"I don't know who you are," she said, laughing, "but you are not leaving here for a good long time." She locked arms with both of us and pulled us eagerly up the path.

"Shake a leg, now. Come and see the baby!"

Epilogue

THE NEW YEAR. I held my cup in both hands and blew a white cloud of breath as I sat on my favorite stump in front of the cabin. The morning was clear and crisp and almost painfully bright, much like the morning we had said goodbye to Etienne.

Before he died, Etienne had put a ring into my hand. *From your mother,* he'd said. I had slipped it on my little finger for safekeeping and hadn't dared to take it off since that moment, not even for Aunt Judith. I set my cup down now to pull off the ring. My fingers trembled. It was a simple, sturdy band of gold, narrow but surprisingly heavy, and it was engraved inside with five words. *For Emily from Etienne. Toujours.* My mother's wedding ring.

There were tears in my eyes as I looked up. Sometimes the world is so full of beauty that I cannot take it in. The sun had risen halfway up the eastern sky, and its bright rays slanted through the oak and hickory branches. Each rough trunk gleamed with last night's frost, each twig scattered the light in a dazzle of crystals.

All our roots go deep into darkness, I thought, and what long shadows each life casts. But somehow the sun still seeks us out each morning.

I slid the ring carefully back onto my finger. Then I stood and gazed westward, remembering four tall trees lifting one man slowly toward the light.

A NOTE ON HISTORY

DANIEL'S WALK IS A WORK OF FICTION, and the events and characters in it are fictional. Only the character of James Clyman is based on an actual person. Clyman was indeed a respected mountain man, and he truly did travel with a large wagon train from Missouri to Oregon in 1844. Aside from this, all that Clyman says and does in the story was invented by me, the author. Any other similarities of characters here to historical persons is purely accidental.

On the other hand, much of Daniel's experience would be familiar to the emigrants who began to make their homes in the American West in the mid-nineteenth century. The journals of ordinary people—trappers, midwives, soldiers, farming families—all record hardships that most of us now find difficult even to imagine. They endured dangers of sickness, weather, injury, crime, starvation, brutal labor, and, not least of all, distance. Many of them overcame these hardships; many of them did not.

For historical details in this book, I relied on some of the classic sources from and about the era, including the journal of James Clyman and histories by DeVoto, Chittenden, and Morgan. In addition, I found lesser-known journals of the time, along with recent scholarly works (by Clyde Milner et al., by Robert Utley, *Western Historical Quarterly*, and others), that bring balance to the more romantic traditional picture of the emigration era.

As Daniel learns—and as thoughtful observers even in his time recognized—the West was not barren or empty or waiting to be "tamed" or "won." In fact, what was known at the time as the doctrine of Manifest Destiny turned out to be manifestly a disaster for millions of Native American people who lived there. The white settlement of the West came at a price in human lives and misery that is comparable to the Holocaust in Europe, or to the enslavement of black people in the American South. This historical fact is evident in the primary sources, and it's clear in current scholarship. You can see it there for yourself. Unfortunately, it has been ignored too often in literature for children and young people.

I hope *Daniel's Walk* is, first of all, a good yarn about a boy on his way to finding his father and himself. But I also hope that, as a work of American historical fiction, the book lends its weight to the efforts of those who are trying to tell a more realistic history and to promote a more humane understanding of how high a price was paid to spread our hungry nation from sea to shining sea.